The Therapist Decides

By Terry Masters

First Published 2023

Copyright © AB Discovery 2023

All rights reserved.

Stories were submitted by various authors to Big Baby World, then edited by Mikey of BBW and published by BBW. Now these have been re-edited by Terry Master and Mikey of Unicorn Tales and published by AB Discovery.

These stories were originally published in the late 1990s but have been updated and edited for your current enjoyment. This volume contains two wonderful full-length stories, "The Therapist Decides" and "Promises, Promises".

Title: The Therapist Decides

Author: Terry Masters

Editor: Michael Bent, Rosalie Bent

Publisher: AB Discovery

© 2023

www.abdiscovery.com.au

Table of Contents

The Therapist Decides 7

An Idea Forms...7

Robert Is Sucked In 13

The Devious Duo Plot Robert's Demise.............................. 17

Robert's Retraining Begins.. 23

Turn Up The Heat.. 31

Success Begins - Slowly... 35

The Plot Thickens 41

Nicky Joins the Plot 45

Robbie is Diapered 49

Robbie Learns The New Rules 59

The Next Step In Robbie's Regression................................. 63

Robbie Becomes A Real Baby 69

Promises, Promises 81

And So It Begins... 81

Baby Davey's Nursery 87

Sissy Baby Davy is Exposed.. 93

Resigned to Being the Sissy Baby Cuckhold......................107

The Therapist Decides

Submitted to BBW in 1998, edited by Terry Master

An Idea Forms

Doctor Patricia Neeland slumped back in her chair, her eyes staring unfocused across the expanse of her office. Her last patient, a fifteen-year-old boy who had been sent to her after he started wetting the bed for no apparent physical reason, had stormed out of the office halfway into the fifty-minute session when her questions became too embarrassing for him to handle. On any other day, she would have pursued him and coaxed him back onto the couch. Today, though, she welcomed the longer interval before her noon group therapy session for troubled teens. Today, she needed the time to sort out her own feelings about what had happened the night before.

It had been a typical night, ending as it usually did with her and her live-in boyfriend of three years snuggling together in bed. She could sense his discomfort, though, a tension running through the muscles of his body. It wasn't like him to keep anything from her, and a simple prompt asking if everything was okay opened the gates.

Robert was a freelance copy editor who worked out the home they shared, having set up a small office in the corner of their den. That afternoon he was doing battle with a stubborn author who took issue with the changes he had made to her novel to better conform with the publisher's norms. He couldn't tell the unfortunate writer that he actually agreed with her arguments without losing his job, so he was stuck defending positions that didn't represent his own views. He had just hung up the phone and was attempting to calm himself down when the doorbell rang. Normally he would ignore it while working, but he needed the distraction. Striding quickly to the foyer, he flung the door open.

It was Joyce, a neighbor from down the street. Robert and Patricia didn't really count her among their friends, having only chatted briefly at block parties. They knew her more from the rumors that swirled through the neighborhood gossip channels which pegged Joyce as a tramp and man-stealer. To hear the worst of it, she had had affairs with no fewer than three married neighbors that led to two divorces. Probably an exaggeration, but who knew?

It was that reputation, deserved or not, that sent nervous tremors through Robert's body when he saw Joyce standing before him. In Robert's recounting of what happened next, Joyce invited herself in and before he knew it, they were sitting at the kitchen table having coffee. Not far from the truth, Patricia thought, knowing how timid Robert was and how easily he could be manipulated. An aggressive woman would have him eating out of her hands in no time.

The purpose, or pretext, of Joyce's visit was to find the name of a reliable plumber. She had an emergency and needed someone better than the last plumber she called. She didn't have phone numbers of any of the neighbors, so she just started knocking on doors, and wasn't it her good fortune that Robert had answered? Robert provided the name of a plumber, but Joyce had questions about his credentials, which led to stories about toilet disasters, which somehow morphed into Robert bemoaning his latest problems with the recalcitrant author.

Whatever plumbing emergency existed couldn't have been that urgent, as an hour quickly flew by as they talked. Robert never noticed that Joyce's chair had gradually shifted closer to his, and he jumped in surprise as she put her hand on his shoulder. Soon it moved to his thigh. She might just be one of those people who talk with their hands, he had explained to Patricia, but he wasn't sure. At that point, his cell phone rang and the irate publisher on the other end of the call demanded his immediate attention, so he swiftly led Joyce to the door.

Was she flirting with him, he asked Patricia that night, *or was it his imagination? Should he have done something sooner?*

Robert stammered out the questions without waiting for answers, and Patricia recognized the signs of guilt. Something more was bothering him, so she ventured a guess. Was there a part of him that welcomed Joyce's attention? Robert blanched, and Patricia had her answer even before he spoke. Yes, he said, he was flattered in a way. But he would never, never act on it. She had to believe him.

And Patricia did believe him, but that didn't make her any less upset. Just because she was a psychologist didn't make her any more rational than anyone else would be in that situation. She said some things she shouldn't have and cried and yelled, and in the end, sent Robert to sleep in the spare bedroom. She snuck out of the house early in the morning to avoid seeing him until she knew that she would have something cogent to say about the situation. He had already called twice, but she allowed the calls to go to voice mail.

Let him sweat!

She knew she had been too harsh with him. He did open up to her and she had no doubt that he had told the full story. But she also didn't want to take any chances that Joyce, or someone just like her, would someday take advantage of the man. Patricia was his first real relationship—he was several years younger than herself--- and he was more like a boy than a man in some ways in knowing how to deal with women. He was naïve and childlike in so many ways, in fact, but that was part of his charm. He was also attentive, loving, and devoted in a way that no prior man had ever been. He and Patricia seemed to fit together perfectly, and she was not about to lose him to some trollop. And she knew that she was a jealous enough type of person that one affair would be enough for her to dump him forever.

Not that any affair he had would last long once the woman got him into bed. Patricia smiled at the image. Robert didn't know it—he was a virgin when Patricia deflowered him—but he was a woeful lover. His penis was small, which wasn't in itself a bad thing, but he didn't make up for the lack of size with any special skill. And he was the poster boy for premature ejaculation. In and over in less than two minutes.

Most women would be frustrated with their lover's lack of performance, but for Patricia, it was one more reason to keep Robert close. When she was barely a teenager, a boy whom she thought was a friend overpowered her and took advantage of her. It was violent and disturbing and left Patricia emotionally scarred. Her parents refused to believe her, her school counselor covered it up and there was no one to help her work through the serious issues she had as a result of the incident.

It was that lack of support that led her to become a child psychologist. Perhaps she could offer help to tortured young souls that she never got. The irony, Patricia knew, was that despite all of her education and supposed wisdom, she could never cure herself of her inner demons. Sex, to her, was unpleasant and unnecessary to her fulfillment as a person. That's why Robert's infrequent quickies were a positive thing. She could never satisfy any man with a healthy sex drive and any penetration for longer than a few minutes would be horrific. She needed to keep him close.

There was one more reason that she could not imagine life without Robert - Nicole, her seventeen-year-old daughter. Despite the circumstances under which she was conceived, she loved Nicole deeply and devoted her life to her. Robert came along just as Nicky was entering into the difficult teenage years and having him as a sort of father figure helped keep her daughter on the right path. Mostly, anyway. He was a good influence on her, and Patricia shuddered to think what would happen if he left their life. Which brought her full circle back to her dilemma.

Kicking Robert out of the house was never an option, and in reality, he didn't do anything wrong. Still, Patricia had to think of a way to prevent any chance of a repeat performance. Since she couldn't count on the boy to recognize the signs of seduction in time to cut them off, the obvious choice was to make him undesirable to other women. But how? What could she do that would maintain his attractiveness to her while putting him off limits to others?

An image of her last patient flashed through her mind, and an idea took root. In an instant, an entire plan formed in Patricia's mind.

It was a bit extreme, more than a little devious, but at first glance, it would be exactly what the doctor ordered. There was no time to consider details, as she could hear her group of unruly teenagers gathering in the waiting area. But it would work. A sudden peacefulness filled Patricia's mind as she got up to open the door.

Patricia used the time during her drive home that evening to fill in the details of her plan and to look at it from every angle. It was deceptively simple, which meant fewer chances of something going wrong. But there were definitely a few possible bumps that could derail the whole thing, and she had to temper her enthusiasm. For one thing, the whole plot hung on her ability to dust off an old skill that she had learned as a tool for her therapy but which she rarely used. She was confident that it wouldn't take long to get back up to speed, however, and if things went according to plan, Robert would knowingly subject himself to it anyway. If it took longer than she expected to bring him under her spell, the delay would be frustrating but would not spoil anything. Besides, knowing him, he would be so willing to please her that she could succeed even as she got back into her rhythm.

The bigger concern was Nicky. She would need to be informed early on about what was going on and at a later point might even need to be involved. Patricia frowned. Would she think her mom had totally lost her mind? Would she reveal everything to Robert in order to protect him? Not likely. Nicky had resisted the authority Patricia gave Robert over her daughter and it was clear that Robert's lack of parenting experience made him timid with her, even as he tried to enforce discipline. There was a bigger chance that Nicky would tell him what Patricia had planned if she thought he would take offense and move out. She was an intelligent girl, and the thought would occur to her. But would she risk alienating her mother and actively take away a true source of happiness for her?

Possibly, but probably not. For one thing, Nicky would be leaving for college in the Fall and would more likely focus on the fact that she would not be under Robert's roof much longer. An even stronger reason, though, was that there would be a heavy dose of humiliation on Robert's part and Nicky would eagerly anticipate being a witness to it. The more she considered Nicky's possible reaction, the more convinced Patricia was that she would enthusiastically support the whole plan - maybe too much. She might actually try to take things to a level beyond what even Patricia intended. She would have to be watched as things unfolded.

By the time she pulled into her driveway, Patricia was not only convinced that she should immediately move forward with her plans but had practiced her initial speech for Robert. She was never one to procrastinate. The minute she walked into that house, it was game on. Robert's life would start changing that very night.

Robert Is Sucked In

Robert was hiding in the den, pretending to be hard at work in order to avoid Patricia, which was fine with her. She needed to talk to her daughter before confronting Robert and starting him on the program that would protect him from the advances of other women. If he knew what was in store for him, she thought smiling, he might not wait so meekly to see how Patricia would be following up on their heated exchange from the night before.

Patricia found Nicole on her bed, listening to music. She looked up questioningly as her mom entered the room. Patricia knew that nothing got by Nicky, and she almost certainly had heard the argument, or at least the raised voices. It was a sign of how mature she was getting that she didn't raise the subject on her own but waited until her mother was ready to talk. It made things easier.

"So how much did you hear last night?" Patricia asked with a soft smile as she sat on the end of the bed. "We were probably pretty loud."

"I heard you yelling, but didn't make out any of the words," Nicky responded. Patricia could tell she was dying of curiosity but wasn't pushing for an explanation. "It isn't like you to scream at him like that."

"No, it isn't, and I apologize that you had to hear that. A child should never have to get in the middle of her parents' disputes." Patricia winced at her own words. Careful now, she told herself, don't go all "therapist" on her. She took a breath and continued. "And really, I should be apologizing to Robert as well. I overreacted."

Patricia then replayed the entire argument for Nicky, being careful to stress that Robert had been forthright and that her own anger at Joyce had been misdirected at him. She explained how important he was to her and how devastating it would be if she lost him, whether to another woman or in any other way. Patricia looked

13

into Nicky's eyes, hoping that she was getting the message that nothing that was being said in that room, woman to woman, was to be used as a device to get him to leave. Nicky looked sincerely saddened at her mother's distress, which was a positive sign. Patricia paused before getting to the heart of why she was there, silently evaluating whether she should open up after all.

Nicky assumed that Patricia was done speaking and used her silence to jump into the conversation. "So, Mom, if what you say is true and you need to apologize to Robert, why are you here talking with me?"

Patricia smiled. Astute girl, she thought. She looked directly at her daughter, made up her mind to follow her original plan, and spoke with confidence. "Because I've decided not to apologize to him. I need to be proactive to make sure that he isn't lured into a situation that will divide us, and for that I need him to think that I'm still angry at him. I have a plan, and I need your help."

Nicole's eyes grew wide, and her mouth opened as if to say something, but she remained mute. Clearly, her first reaction was one of surprise and probably a little bit of shock that her own mother would consider something apparently a bit sinister. Then her face changed. Patricia didn't need to be a psychologist to see that Nicky was excited. As she expected, the idea of conspiring against Robert was clearly thrilling to Nicky. Her daughter's next words confirmed this.

"So, what are we going to do? When are we going to start?"

Patricia giggled a bit at Nicky's obvious enthusiasm, which caused Nicky to giggle and soon mother and daughter were laughing together. Patricia composed herself, moved closer to Nicky, and took her by the hand.

"You have to understand that what I'm about to tell you, what we're going to do, has to be absolutely confidential. You can't tell anyone, not even Sarah," she said, referring to Nicky's best friend since kindergarten. "I could not only lose Robert but lose my license."

Nicky nodded solemnly. She sat attentively, waiting for Patricia to continue. Patricia hesitated, suddenly unsure of how to start. She decided to build to it slowly.

"I trust Robert. I think his heart is true in his affection for and loyalty to me. I don't really believe he would betray me willingly. It's just that he's, well, he's, shall we say, a bit naïve when it comes to certain things." Patricia didn't miss Nicky's fleeting smile. Her own daughter was more aware of the trappings of the sexual world than her boyfriend, who was a decade older, and Nicky knew it.

"So ,it's not enough to get his assurances that it won't happen again, and I can't always be around to protect him from the predators like Joyce. I can't exactly sprinkle a magic powder on him to make him more aware. The whole episode from yesterday has convinced me that the only way I can feel safe is to make Robert unappealing to other women."

Nicky's face first flushed with puzzlement as she tried to work out where her mom was going, then cleared as she nodded. "I guess that makes sense. But what could you do? You can't exactly splash acid on his face or anything."

"No, I wasn't talking about his physical appearance. I was thinking something completely different." Nicky looked confused again as Patricia tried to think of a way to approach the subject in a way that she would understand. Then an idea hit her. "Do you remember last summer when you babysat the Jordans' daughter? How cute you thought she was when you first picked her up?"

Nicky's eyes rolled up at the memory. "She was cute. A little dolly. But I don't understand..." Nicky stopped mid-sentence as she suddenly saw where her mom was going. Her mouth dropped open and she looked at Patricia with a combination of surprise and amazement. "You can't be serious."

"It was the first time you had sat for a child that young. I remember you took a picture of her on your phone and sent it to me with a message talking about how adorable she was, and how perfect her little fingers and toes and nose were. You were gushing so much I was worried that you would run out afterward ready to have one of your own."

Nicky snickered. "Yes, and then she fouled her diaper and she wasn't so cute anymore. She was wet and stinky, and it was disgusting. I think I was crying when I called you."

"Yes, and if you remember I had to come over to change the diaper. That was the last time you babysat for her. You thought she was the prettiest thing you had ever seen, but that all changed in a moment. The baby's appearance didn't change, just your perception of her. You went from wanting to keep her for yourself to never wanting to be near her again."

"I remember. I get it now. But it's not like you can get Robert to wear diapers," Nicky said jokingly. Patricia blushed as her lips curled into a devilish smile. She nodded and Nicky stared at her in admiration and excitement. "But how? You need to tell me everything and you need to tell me now!"

And for the next thirty minutes, Patricia did just that.

The Devious Duo Plot Robert's Demise

Before leaving Nicole's room, Patricia had to caution her daughter again about the importance of keeping everything they had discussed to herself. The girl was so excited about their plans that she was literally bouncing on the bed. For her, it was Christmas in July.

As she reached the bottom of the stairs, Patricia breathed a sigh of relief. One hurdle cleared without a problem. The next one, though, was much more critical. Even though Robert was not as perceptive as Nicky, one false move would still make him suspicious and that would ruin everything. There was no turning back at this point, though, so Patricia steeled herself and strode toward the den.

Patricia could feel Robert tense up as she entered the room. The fact that he was nervous in her presence, perhaps even a bit scared, was a positive thing. She needed him to be willing to do whatever it would take to repair their relations, and it helped if he still thought that she was angry with him. He would have to put his fate in her hands of his own accord.

"Robert, we need to talk." Patricia hoped that he didn't notice the slight tremor in her voice, or that he would assume it was a result of her continuing irritation with him. He turned to face her, and at that moment Patricia knew she was going to succeed. He was pale, trembling, and had the look of a prisoner being led to his execution. Putty in her hands.

"Patricia, I'm sorry. Really, I am. I didn't realize—"

"Stop right there, Robert." Patricia cut him off deliberately. She didn't want to give him the chance to launch into whatever speech of contrition he had been rehearsing all day. She had to assume control of the course of the conversation. "I've been thinking about what happened yesterday and I know it wasn't entirely your fault. Joyce took advantage of your good nature. But the fact that you let it go as far as you did, even if it was subconsciously, worries me. I think it may reflect uncertainties that you have about our relationship, that maybe on some level you are looking to see what else is out there. Deep down, your commitment might not be as strong as you think it is. That concerns me."

"But Pat, you don't—"

"Robert, don't interrupt. I'm trained to analyze just these kinds of behaviors and no matter what you say, I'm sure I'm right to be worried. If I'm to forgive you for your actions yesterday, if we are to continue as a couple, I need to make sure that you aren't harboring thoughts of other women. I've come up with a way that I can overcome any doubts I have about your level of devotion. Unless you agree, I could never be completely comfortable in my own mind. In that case, you might as well pack your bags and go tonight."

Patricia waited for a reaction. Robert's posture reminded her of a deflated balloon. The temptation to soften her words was enormous, but she needed to remain cross to effectuate his upcoming training. "Robert, that was your cue to speak. Are you willing to do what I ask in order to keep us together?" Robert was so overcome with emotion at that point, she doubted that he realized she never told him anything about what she was asking him to agree to.

"Of course, dear, I would do anything. You have to know that I love you and would never even think about leaving you." Patricia saw the light bulb go off in his head and he looked at her with a puzzled expression. "Um, what exactly is it that you need me to do?"

"First, I think it's best if we don't share the same bed for a while until all of my doubts have been erased. You can use Nicky's old bedroom." No protests so far. Good. "Next, since my biggest concerns involve your subconscious desires, the part of your mind that harbors thoughts that even you don't realize, I want to probe that area of your brain. I want to see if there's anything in there that shouldn't be. In other words, I want to hypnotize you."

Robert's jaw dropped, and a slight squeak may have emitted from his mouth, but he didn't say a word. Patricia didn't want to give him a chance to object, so she kept on going.

"It's the only way I can address my doubts. If your subconscious mind reveals the sort of love and devotion that you claim you have…" She gave him a stern look, hopefully conveying the impression that she had her doubts about the sincerity of his protestations, "then we're good and can move on with confidence. If not, well, then…" Patricia let Robert fill in the rest in his mind.

"So, starting tonight, every evening before bedtime we will spend some time together answering our questions." Patricia wanted Robert to think that this was a mutual undertaking. "You will get comfortable, and I'll gently put you into a trance, where your innermost thoughts will reveal themselves to me. I'll be the one doing all of the work. You will probably come to enjoy these times. I've heard they're very relaxing.

"It's not something that can be done in a single night or even a week. I won't know how long it will take to get the answers I need. I have many, many questions."

As she said this, Patricia moved over to where Robert sat dazed in his chair and stood above him menacingly. It had all gone just as she had hoped. He was so overwhelmed with guilt and confusion that she had run him over before he could form any thoughts of his own. As far as he knew, her anger from the night before had not abated one bit.

"Now, you can get back to work. Dinner in thirty minutes."

Dinner was uncomfortable, which was exactly how Patricia wanted it to be. She had to keep Robert thinking she was still upset with him so that the warmth she would show later if the hypnotic triggers worked would reinforce the desired behaviors. Nicky played the role of the sullen teenager perfectly, although more than once Patricia saw her glance at her stepfather with a subtle grin.

When he had finished eating, Robert slunk from the table and retreated to the den, closing the door behind him. Patricia had barely got up to clear the table when Nicky burst out excitedly.

"Well, how did it go? Is everything okay? Did he agree to let you hypnotize him? When are you going to start?"

The questions spilled from her daughter's mouth faster than Patricia could answer them. She finally sat back down and faced her daughter.

"Shhh… not so loud. Yes, he agreed. I didn't leave him much choice. We are going to start tonight."

Nicky smiled widely. "Do you think it's going to work right away? I mean, will he wet the bed tonight?" Patricia was a bit taken aback by her daughter's enthusiasm. Then again, she anticipated the idea of humiliating her Stepdad would appeal to Nicky.

"It's possible—he's pretty suggestible—but it will probably take several sessions. We'll just have to wait and see. And no," Patricia could see the next question form in Nicky's mind, "you can't listen in. I need to be able to concentrate without having to worry about you making a noise."

She could tell that Nicky was momentarily disappointed, but it didn't take long before she regained her excitement. After all, the process itself was not the best part, The result was what would make it fun for her.

Patricia's own vocalization that she would be starting that very night brought on an unexpected case of nerves. She would need a few minutes to gain her composure and build up her confidence, but first, she decided to make sure Nicky knew her own role.

"Now, you do know how you're supposed to act around Robert in the normal course of the day, right? I'm going to tell him that you and I had a talk and that you are aware that we are having problems. You'll need to be distant and cold. He'll assume that you have taken my side in our difficulty and are upset with his behavior." As she spoke, Patricia realized that "*distant and cold*" wasn't a whole lot different from how Nicky usually interacted with Robert, so she wouldn't need to put on a performance. "But if he has an accident during his sleep, and you discover it, tell me what you need to do."

If she was exasperated at her mother's covering the same ground for the hundredth time, Nicole didn't show it. "I am to be sickeningly sympathetic to him, and to be really nice, and to let him know that it could happen to anyone. And to give him a hug and treat him like I care." Nicky frowned as she spoke. Patricia also frowned; those weren't quite her words, but the gist of it was accurate enough.

"Close enough. Basically, the only time either you or I will show Robert any warmth is when he is wet. Hopefully, that will plant the right idea in his subconscious."

Nicky giggled a bit, and Patricia reached over and put her hand over that of her daughter. "Well, wish me luck. I need to get things rolling."

Patricia stood outside the door to the den for a few moments, closed her eyes, and muttered a simple mantra intended to give her a confidence she didn't feel. After a couple of deep breaths, she entered the room.

Robert was startled at her approach and quickly turned to face Patricia as she pulled a chair over close to his. He seemed to sense that she did not want him to say a word, for which she was grateful.

"I just had a long talk with Nicole." She saw the protest rise in Robert's eyes and rushed to continue before he could object. "She would have wondered what was going on between us. Kids sense these things. Especially with us sleeping in separate bedrooms.

"As you might expect, she wasn't happy. You might find it a bit uncomfortable in her presence for a few days, but she'll get over it. What you have to be concerned about more is whether I will get over it. As unorthodox as it may seem for me to probe your mind... and believe me I feel as weird about it as you probably do... it really does seem to be the only path to restoring the trust I once had in you.

"I'm anxious to get started so that we can move forward as quickly as possible. I know you've been tense all day—I can feel it even now—but to put you into a deep hypnotic state I'll need you to be entirely relaxed before I even begin. Go to your room, I mean Nicky's old bedroom, and lay down on the bed. Close your eyes. Try to put all of the day's events out of your mind as much as possible. There are a few things I need to do to prepare, but I'll be in shortly. Now go."

Robert left, obeying her instructions without comment or question. Patricia exhaled as he climbed the stairs, unaware that she had been holding her breath. She turned to the computer, signed on to her private account, and began to search websites for the items that she would be needing soon if all went well.

After about an hour, as darkness began to fall, she left the den and ascended the stairs, ready to begin Robert's regression.

Robert's Retraining Begins

Patricia was surprised to see Robert lying peacefully on the bed, sleeping. He probably hadn't slept much the night before, she thought. Before waking him, she pulled a chair up close to the side of the bed and glanced around the room. Nicky had moved out several years before, but it still had all the fittings of a pre-teen's dream. Pink, frilly bed cover and matching curtains, boy band posters on the walls, and stuffed animals littered here and there. Patricia smiled slightly. Too bad it didn't still have her crib and changing table.

Patricia shook Robert's shoulder gently, instructing him to remain quiet and to sit up with his back propped up against the pillows. She deliberately kept the lights dim. The hypnotic trance would be easier to induce if he remained a bit sleepy.

"Now, Robert, I want you to cooperate with me on this. I know you're going to want to try to analyze everything I'm saying, and you'll be tempted to pretend to fall into a trance in order to keep control over your answers, but I would be able to tell. I would not be happy and such behavior would be evidence that you're hiding something that you don't want me to know. If you understand, nod your head."

Robert nodded. After all of the planning and plotting, it was finally time to begin.

"Now I want you to look past my shoulder and look at the corner of the room, where the ceiling and the walls meet. Focus on that spot. Do not let your eyes wander away from that spot. As we go along, if you find that your eyes are getting heavy and it is too much work to keep them open, you may close your eyes, but keep them looking right in the direction of that corner even as your eyelids close.

"I want you to imagine yourself sitting on the side of a hill in a field full of flowers. The sun is shining, and a light breeze is blowing. The flowers sway gently in the wind. You can just

23

barely smell the sweet scent of the flowers and it pleases
you. The sun is warm, and you are very calm and happy in
the field. The warmth of the sun, the feeling of the breeze
on your cheek, and the scent of the flowers, all come
together to make this a very pleasant place. You lay back,
nestling into the flowers, letting the sun warm your entire
body.

"You close your eyes, and as you do so a feeling of heaviness
begins to descend upon you. It is a pleasant sensation, and
you allow it to happen. It starts at the top of your head. You
realize that your head is very heavy, and you could not lift it
if you wanted to, but you do not want to. Your eyelids rest
closed. They, too, are heavy. It is as if there are weights
attached to your eyelids. You try to open your eyes, but they
are too heavy. Try, now, Robert, try to gently open your
eyes."

In his sleepy state, Robert had closed his eyes almost as soon
as Patricia began talking, but dutifully kept them faced toward the
corner of the wall. She watched as his eyelids flickered, but his eyes
remained shut. So far, so good.

"The heaviness moves down now toward your shoulders
and your chest. Your body and the ground seem to be one.
Your arms now weigh hundreds of pounds, maybe more.
You cannot lift them. Try, Robert, try to lift your arms."

As with his eyes, Robert made an effort to raise his arms, but
they stayed at his sides. Patricia continued down his body until she
had him feeling like he was totally unable to move. Next step.

"As you lay in the field, the warm sun upon you, an escalator
appears before you. This makes perfect sense to you, and
you find yourself standing at the top of the escalator. You
want to take it down. You want to descend deeper, and
deeper into your subconscious. You step on, and the stairs
begin to take you downward. With each passing count, from
ten to one, you go deeper and deeper into sleep, but you
will still hear my voice. Ten..."

Patricia brought Robert slowly down to "one," and then repeated the descent with an elevator. She was certain that Robert had long before passed into a deep trance, but she wanted to make sure. She lifted his arm and was pleased as it fell, offering no resistance. She tested him in a couple of different ways and was finally convinced that he was ready.

At this stage, she paused. While it wasn't strictly true that you could not hypnotize someone to do something that they didn't want to do, the suggestion would be much stronger and more effective if the subject thought that it was their idea to perform the suggested task. She would have to proceed cautiously.

"Robert, while you are in this trance-like state, I don't want you to think of me as your girlfriend, or even as someone you know. I am more like a wise spirit who is here to help you with any problems that are bothering you, and to guide you to a solution. If you understand me, I want you to raise your right index finger."

Patricia was pleased to see his finger rise, and it encouraged her to continue.

"I can tell that you are under stress and that something has happened that confuses you. If that is correct, raise your finger. Good. Together we will be working on finding a way to fix this, to find a path to make everything better. Can you do that with me?"

Again, the finger. Time to move on, to let him verbalize.

"Now, Robert, I want you to tell me in just a few words what is making you so tense."

Robert's face scrunched in thought and for a moment Patricia wondered if she had pushed him too fast. Then again, all day he worked with words and was probably trying to think of how he could concisely convey his situation. She was relieved when he spoke.

"My girlfriend is angry with me."

"Good, Robert, very good. That gives us a place to start. Do you know why she is angry with you? Remember, just a few words."

"She doesn't trust me."

"*Good, very good,*" Patricia kept her voice soft yet in command. "*Now, Robert, it is very hard for a man to regain a woman's trust, but I know how to do it. I have a way that has never failed, but it is not an easy thing for most men to do. Most men fail to show a strong enough commitment to the woman to follow my advice because it is hard. Tell me, Robert, do you care enough about this woman to do something that will not be easy for you? Are you committed enough to her to follow my plan no matter how strange or difficult it might seem?*"

Patricia could have kicked herself. It violated hypnotic principles to ask multiple questions without waiting for an answer. She needn't have worried.

"Yes, yes, I will do anything for her. No matter what it is."

Patricia closed her eyes for a moment and had to pause. Poor Robert was a good and devoted man. Did she really want to put him through this? An image of Joyce flashed through her mind, and that was enough to steel her to go on.

"*I believe you, Robert. I believe that you will do anything for her. I will help you regain her trust. You would like that, wouldn't you, Robert? You would do anything for you?*" Patricia panicked for a moment when he didn't respond, then smiled when she noticed his finger pointing skyward.

"*The first step, Robert, is to change her perception of you, to see you as someone who would never knowingly hurt her. We need her to see you as the picture of innocence, as someone who loves her unconditionally and one who is incapable of intentionally inflicting pain. Can you think of what kind of person that would be?*"

Robert remained quiet and appeared puzzled, as Patricia expected. She pushed on.

"*You want her to know that even if you are a little naughty, or do something unpleasant, it was not done on purpose. There are women who show unlimited love toward such other people even when they seem to misbehave, and they are not angry. Is that what you want, Robert?*"

No finger this time; Robert's head was nodding so vigorously that Patricia worried he would wake himself up.

"Yes, Robert, that's what you want and also what you need. Do you know what these women are called, Robert?" A slight head shake. "They are called mothers. Women who have children, little children, love their children more than anything even if the child does a naughty thing, because children don't know any better. Isn't that right?"

Another nod, but also obvious puzzlement. She needed to connect the dots quickly before he started thinking on his own rather than adopting her suggestions.

"That's right, Robert. We need her to see you as she sees a child, someone who may not always behave but who doesn't know any better. The first step to regaining her trust is to suggest that you could never do anything to hurt her on purpose. Does that make sense to you, Robert?"

Robert nodded again, and a slight smile spread across his face. I'm glad this makes sense to you, Robert, Patricia thought, because to me it is clearly a pile of shit.

"Do you trust me to help you with this, Robert?" A firm nod. "Good. Here is what you need to do. You don't even need to remember that you need to do this. I am addressing your subconscious here. Your subconscious will remember for you, okay? Tonight, and every night from now on, you need to do just one little thing that only children do so that she will see you as innocent and loving, just like a child. Robert, you will start wetting your bed in your sleep. When you are deeply asleep, when your mind is at rest and your subconscious takes over, it will tell you to release your bladder and wet yourself in your sleep. You will not wake up to do this. In fact, the act of urinating will send you into a deeper sleep and you will not awaken until morning. Can you do this for her, Robert?"

Robert nodded, although less than enthusiastically.

"Good, Robert. Very good. You will see. Just this one child-like act will begin to break down the barriers. It will make

her see you differently, and she will begin to love you as she loves a child. She will trust you and she will love you."

Patricia continued for a bit longer, reinforcing the suggestion and stressing the reward, being careful to always associate her love and trust with the actions of a child. Listening to herself she became doubtful that this would work. It all sounded so ridiculous. Still, she knew that subjects under hypnosis were much more suggestible, and Robert wanted to make up so badly that maybe he really would do this. Only time would tell.

Patricia paused, took a breath, and began to slowly bring Robert out of his trance. As soon as he awoke, she stood up and exited the room.

Patricia slept poorly that night. She felt drained from the strain of the hypnotic session with Robert and the interrogation from Nicky that followed. Still, her emotional exhaustion did not translate into actual sleepiness, and she could not get her mind to relax. Would Robert really wake up wet? And if he did, what next? Could she go through with her plan or was the whole thing just absurd? Frustrated, she watched the minutes tick by on her bedside clock until sometime after 4:00 a.m. she fell into a restless sleep.

Tired as she was, Patricia bolted out of bed at 7:00 a.m. Not surprisingly, she found her normally late-sleeping daughter already up and eating breakfast in the kitchen. No words had to be exchanged. Patricia poured a cup of coffee for herself and sat down across from Nicky, who eventually broke the silence.

"How are you going to do this? If I wet the bed, I don't think I would tell you. You need to go in and check."

Patricia nodded wearily. "I know. Wait until I finish my coffee. He usually doesn't get up until closer to 8:00 anyway."

Patricia knew she was stalling, afraid of what she might find when she checked up on Robert. She wasn't even sure what result she was hoping for. If he was dry, doubt would creep in about whether she had the ability to make him lose his continence. If he was wet, she wasn't sure she had the energy for the next stage.

Wearily, she got up and headed upstairs. Nicky began to follow but sat back down after Patricia shook her head. It wasn't time to bring her into the picture yet.

Patricia cursed as she tried to quietly open the door to her daughter's former room. Damn, she thought, why is it she had never noticed how squeaky the floor was or how the door creaked when she opened it? Peeking in, she was relieved to see Robert slumbering with his front side facing the door. Patricia sniffed the air for any telltale sign of an accident but could detect nothing. She slowly bent down until her face was level with the bed, pulled the sheet covering Robert up with two fingers, and looked intently at the bed near his crotch.

Nothing. The sheets were dry as a bone. She didn't see the slightest sign of moisture on his pajama bottoms. Disappointment crushed her. It took all of her energy to straighten up and walk slowly back out of the room, closing the door behind her.

Nicky did not take the news well. "Do you think you did something wrong? Is there somewhere online you can get help? What are you doing to do now? You're not going to give up, are you?"

Patricia couldn't help but smile at her daughter's assumption that the internet was a magical place where you could find the answers to any question, even how to hypnotize your special someone into peeing himself in his sleep.

"I told you that it wasn't very likely to work with only one session. Robert knows that last night was not a one-time thing. I'll be putting him under every day until we either get results or have to assume that it's not going to work. In the meantime, we have to continue acting as we have been. I'm the angry girlfriend and you're my sullen and distant daughter."

Nicole stuck her tongue out at her mom and soon they were both giggling, breaking the tension. Still, Patricia could see the disappointment her daughter felt, and she felt a strong maternal urge not to let her down again. A new determination surged through her body, and she just knew that she had to make this work. She took Nicky's hand and looked her straight in the eyes.

"This will work. I'll make it work. I promise."

Nicky immediately looked like a burden had been lifted and Patricia was relieved. She grabbed her briefcase and headed out the door.

Damn it, she thought. *Now I've got to get results. But how?*

Turn Up The Heat

How, indeed!

Every unoccupied moment, and even occasionally during sessions, Patricia focused on her words to Robert the night before. She had been deliberately cautious, but was she too careful? She had tried to make Robert think that wetting as a means of getting sympathy was his idea, but he hadn't made the connection, so she had had to come right out and say it. Had she been too direct? On the contrary, she thought, she probably hadn't been direct enough. By the end of the day, she had her plan in place. She simply had to be a little more obvious as to the behavior she expected and hope that his subconscious was willing to accept her suggestions.

Robert was already lying on the guest bed when Patricia entered the room later that night. Compliant as always, she thought, but he had probably also enjoyed the restful feeling of being in a trance. Someone had once told her that an hour under hypnosis was the equivalent of getting a full night's sleep.

He wasn't sleeping, but again it didn't take much effort to get him deep into a hypnotic state. Patricia covered some of the same ground as the first session, allowing Robert to express his frustration at the rift in his relationship. She pushed a bit more this time on getting him to admit that he would do anything to fix it. By the time she was ready to move into the suggestion part of their time, he would have jumped off a bridge if she asked him to.

"Robert, remember how we talked about your becoming more childlike? How the way back into your girlfriend's heart is by triggering her maternal instincts? You were going to wet the bed for me, Robert. You were going to act like a small child in order to start the process of reconciliation. It's a small step but an important one. Did you do that for me, Robert? Did you wet the bed?"

31

A deep crease spread across Robert's brow as he frowned. "No. I'm sorry but I didn't do it."

Patricia needed to reinforce his awareness of the behavior she was asking of him. "Didn't do what, Robert? What didn't you do?"

"I didn't wet the bed."

"That's disappointing to me, Robert. I thought we were going to work together to repair your relationship with Patricia. All I asked of you was one little thing. All I asked you to do was to wet the bed, but you didn't do it. I thought you wanted my help, Robert. Maybe you don't want me to help you after all."

Patricia felt mean as Robert's face reflected his panic. "No! I mean, yes! I want your help. I need your help. I'm sorry. Please don't leave me."

Patricia felt a tear form in the corner of her eye. His dependence on others already made him so much like a child. She wanted to hug him, to tell him that everything would be okay. But it wouldn't be okay, not unless she continued. As cruel as this might seem, this really was for his own good.

"I'm still here, Robert," she said softly. "Let's work this out together. I gave you one simple task. Do you know why you didn't follow my advice?"

He shook his head slightly. "I don't know. You have to believe me."

"I do believe you, Robert. I'm willing to keep trying if you are. Are you willing to keep trying, Robert?"

He nodded his head as a barely audible "yes" escaped his lips.

"All right, Robert. Let's try to go about this in a different way. Let's go back to your childhood, to feel like you are a child again. As I count backward, the years will be slipping away and you will become younger. Are you ready to begin?"

A nod.

"All right, Robert. You are beginning your journey back to when you were a child. All of your adult behaviors are fading

into the background until we need them again. You are no longer thirty years old. You are now twenty-five, now twenty. Feel as the years fall away. You feel younger and more energetic. You like becoming younger. It is a good feeling to lose your adulthood.

Patricia took it slowly, year by year, gauging her boyfriend's reaction as she stripped him of one adult trait after another.

"Robert, you are now barely in your teens, just out of puberty. Your body is awkward, it doesn't always do what you want it to do. You have acne. It is embarrassing. You wake up in the morning and your underpants are crusty from the accidents growing boys have while they sleep. Do you want to stay at this age, Robert?"

She smiled at the vigorous shaking of his head. Puberty is a bitch for all of us, she thought. Who would want to do that twice?

"Then let's go farther back. The years keep falling away. You are now ten, no, now you are nine. You no longer have a man's body. Your penis is small and soft. There is no body hair around it, and you don't need to shave. Your voice is higher, like a girl's voice. Life is so much simpler now. You like being a boy, don't you Robert?

"Let's continue backward. You are now six, now five. It feels so good to be young again. Four, now three. One more year, Robert. Let's go back to when you were two years old. You are a toddler again. Your body is rounder, and you are still learning new skills. Walking is new to you. When you talk, you use only a few simple words. You rely on your mommy to dress you and to feed you. She is a loving mommy and takes care of her little Bobby, doesn't she?"

Patricia was surprised as she gazed into Robert's face. It actually looked younger. A peacefulness enveloped him. He was actually accepting his role as a toddler. But he had been in a trance for a long time now, and she knew its effectiveness would soon be reduced. She had to move forward quickly.

"Your mommy loves you even more when you need her the most, doesn't she Bobby? Let's remember when you woke

up in the morning and something wasn't right. Do you
remember when you woke up in your bed, or your crib, and
your pants were soggy and cold and uncomfortable? You
were a big boy, but you had an accident, and big boys
weren't supposed to have accidents, were they?"

Robert looked like he was going to cry. This was supposed to
be a created memory, but Patricia wondered if she was reminding him
of actual events. She pressed on.

"You are worried that Mommy will be mad. That she won't
be happy with her big boy that wets the bed. Aren't you
Bobby? But when Mommy comes in, she's not angry. She
knows that accidents happen, even to big boys. Mommy
smiles and says that she loves you, and you know that it's
true. She hugs you, helps you take off your big boy
underpants, and cleans you up. She talks to you gently and
holds you close, and she smells so good. She doesn't punish
you. She loves her big boy. Even when he has an accident.
Especially when he has an accident."

Robert looked at peace once more. Time to wrap up. Patricia
took another ten minutes or so to reinforce the idea that accidents
translated into demonstrations of love, then again asked Robert to
have an accident so that Patricia could show him her love. She then
slowly brought him back to his true age, reminded him that he would
remember nothing of what they had discussed while he was under,
and woke him up. By the time he opened up his eyes, she was gone.

Success Begins - Slowly

Disappointment reigned again as Robert remained dry that second morning. And the third. Patricia continued their nightly sessions, but her confidence was beginning to waiver. On the fourth morning, though, he was damp. Not soaked, not even what you would call wet, but he had definitely leaked into his underpants.

This development brought on a spirited debate at breakfast that morning between Patricia and Nicky, who continued to rise early in anticipation of the big moment. Nicky thought it was time to move to phase two, while Patricia thought they needed more.

"I'm sorry, Nicky, but it just wasn't dramatic enough for me to show him that much concern. We need more."

The fifth morning, they got more. As Patricia stealthily snuck into Robert's bedroom, she immediately noticed the strong scent of ammonia in the air. She didn't even need to get close to the bed to assess the damage. The wet sheets were clearly visible from across the room. Quietly, she backed out of the room and closed the door.

Her excitement must have been obvious because she had barely entered the kitchen when Nicky let out a squeal of delight. Patricia had to tell her to hush, but it was an effort to hold their voices down to a whisper as they discussed what to do next.

For all of her planning, Patricia really hadn't thought this step through. Could she trust Robert to confess his accident to her? Should she "accidentally" discover it herself? A quick consultation with her daughter found them in agreement: they couldn't leave anything to chance. Patricia had to go back to Robert's room.

"Now don't forget, Nicky, as far as Robert is concerned you don't know anything about his little problem. It's not time yet to get you involved." Nicky's jubilation immediately gave way to a major pout, but Patricia knew that she would get over it shortly. She kissed her daughter on the top of her head. "Wish me luck."

Patricia heard Robert moving about behind the closed door. Good, she thought, this will make it easier. In one swift movement, she flung open the door.

"Robert, I---" Patricia stopped mid-sentence, only partly feigning astonishment at the sight that greeted her. Robert stood by the side of the bed, sodden sheets bundled in his hands, urine dripping from his pajama bottoms onto the floor. His face immediately turned a bright shade of red while his mouth hung open silently. Patricia knew at that moment that he was going to try to hide the evidence of his misfortune and that she was justified in having decided to intervene.

"Robert, what is going on here?" she said sternly as she crossed over to stand in front of her embarrassed boyfriend. "Did you do what I think you did?"

"Patricia, I'm so sorry. I... I..." Robert stammered for several seconds, clearly flustered and not knowing what to say. It was time for Patricia to come to the rescue.

She reached for the sheets, held one portion to her nose, and sniffed, then gently pushed them to the side for a clear view of Robert's wet pajamas and the small golden puddle at his feet.

"Why, yes you did! Honey, you wet the bed! I'm so sorry, dear, have you been feeling all right? Are you sick?" As she spoke, Patricia pulled Robert's head close to her bosom, stroking it gently before moving her arm around him in a loving, if maternal, fashion.

"What am I doing, making you stand here while I carry on? Just dump those wet things on the bed so that I can get them in the wash before I go to work." As Robert turned to release his pungent load, Patricia knelt down and began to pull his pajama bottoms down. "Now step out, first the right, now the left. Good boy. Now your shirt." Patricia moved his hands away as he went to unbutton his pajama top and moved in closely, intentionally rubbing her breasts against him as she took her time undoing each button, then almost hugging him as she pulled the sleeves down his arms. She added the pajamas to the pile of sheets.

"Oh, look at you, you're shivering. Come with me, let's get you cleaned up." Patricia took the dazed Robert by the hand and led him to the bathroom, where she ran hot water into the sink. Without saying a word, she soaped up a warm, wet washcloth and began to rub it slowly across his groin, taking particular time with his penis. She had to hide a smile as it began to respond, but before he could get too excited, she moved around and began to clean his behind, again spending more time than was necessary to clean his skin of pee. She finished up his legs and feet, then wrapped him in a fluffy towel and dried him herself. Glancing at his face from time to time, she could tell that he was enjoying being pampered.

"There you go, Robert, all better. I need to hurry and get that load in the washer; I'd appreciate it if you would remember to put it in the dryer when it's done. Then I need to get to work. If you're sick, have Nicky go out and get you something to help you out."

Before he could respond, she left him standing naked in the bathroom, no doubt relishing the interaction despite the circumstances that brought it on. With a little more hypnotic prodding, Patricia hoped they would have a repeat performance the next morning.

They did.

While in a trance the night after he had wet the bed, Robert was clearly conflicted. He was terribly humiliated at having acted so childish, but just as obviously cherished the return of the warmer side of the woman he loved. The fact that Patricia never mentioned the incident, and then treated him just as coldly as she had been doing upon her return from work, was not lost on Robert. Patricia didn't even have to suggest the link between his wetting and the exhibition of her gentler, more loving side. She did, however, make sure that Robert's subconscious would see the merit of a repeat performance.

Patricia didn't need to create an excuse to check in on Robert the next morning. While he was under the night before, she implanted the suggestion that he would sleep heavily and late, and she was gratified to see that he barely stirred when she entered his room. The smell of urine was again strong, and she could see the sheets clinging to his pajamas. Patricia bent over the bed and gently shook Robert by the shoulder.

"Robert, honey, wake up. You've had another accident." Robert's eyes opened slowly, still feeling the grogginess of sleep, but then his nose twitched, and his eyes opened wide as the odor and feeling of his nighttime wetting hit him at the same time. He looked up at Patricia with horror in his eyes. She knew it was time to play the role of a loving wife.

"Don't worry, Robbie," she cooed softly, deliberately using a more juvenile form of his name, "these things happen sometimes. Now come along with me and we can get you cleaned up and into some nice clean underpants." Patricia worried a bit that he would object to her more maternal tone of voice but if Robert noticed he didn't object. She again took him by the hand and led him to the bathroom. Improvising, she decided to take things a step further than the previous morning.

Patricia motioned to her boyfriend to sit on the toilet, pushing him lightly on the shoulders as he began to sit. "Now be a big boy and see if you have any pee pee left that you can tinkle into the potty," she said, "while I draw you a warm bath."

Robert opened his mouth to say something, but in the end, remained silent. Patricia assumed correctly that he was reluctant to do or say anything that might bring on the return of the witch he'd been living with lately. To her surprise and delight, she heard the splashing as Robert peed into the bowl.

"Good boy!" she smiled, giving him a hug. "Now let's get you cleaned up and ready for your day." She helped Robert step into the tub, which she had only filled with about four inches of water. As she turned to grab a washcloth, Robert finally found his voice.

"You don't need to do this, Patricia. I can wash myself." His red face clearly betrayed his embarrassment at the whole situation.

"Why of course you can, I know that," she replied warmly. "But what kind of girlfriend would I be if I didn't help out my man when he needs it?" With that, she began washing him, humming lowly as she did so. It took several minutes before she realized she was humming songs she used to sing to Nicole when she was a baby. When she got to his penis, she again spent more time than necessary, stroking it with the soapy washcloth until it began to grow, then stopping.

"Now turn over so that I can get your behind." Robert hesitated but quickly complied when he noticed Patricia's expression begin to cloud over. "That's a good boy. We have to make sure that we get everywhere so that you don't get a rash."

For a moment, Patricia thought about washing his hair but felt that she had pushed things to their limit for that day. She had Robert stand up and step out of the tub, where she proceeded to dry him for the second straight day. She made sure that she was all smiles and sunshine as she completed her task.

"Wait right here," she instructed him before walking swiftly to his dresser. She re-entered the bathroom carrying a pair of his underwear she had pulled from his drawer. Without saying a word, she examined the crotch carefully, even putting it up to her nose for a quick sniff. "I don't see any evidence that you've been having problems during the day, so that's good. But Robert," and here she put her hands on his shoulders, "if this happens again, we're going to have to have a talk about what we can do about it. Do you agree?"

Robert was so overwhelmed by the whole scenario, as well as confused as to why an act that should have brought on Patricia's wrath was instead met with kindness, that he simply nodded.

"Good boy," she said, then she kissed him on the cheek and turned to leave. Robert stood still, dazed, for a full five minutes before he began to get dressed and ready for the day.

The Plot Thickens

Patricia could tell that Robert was disappointed that her warm mood from the morning had not carried over to the rest of the day. This time, the progress that had been made in one day made it much easier for Patricia to feign her continued anger as she was now impatient to move things forward at a fast pace. She was relieved, then, when Robert retreated to his room after dinner and closed the door and she could stop her act as the frosty bitch.

As they were drying the last of the dishes, Patricia caught her daughter's eye and smiled. "We need to talk, Nicky. I think it's time to bring you into the picture."

If there was any doubt about Nicky's level of enthusiasm for Project Robert, it vanished at that moment. Nicky practically jumped up and down as she led her mom by the hand to the kitchen table, almost forcing her to sit in one of the chairs.

"I've been SO waiting for you to say that. First, tell me what's been happening so far," she whispered, her voice trembling in excitement.

Patricia summed up her sessions with Robert and his eventual bed-wetting in short order, smiling as Nicky giggled at the image of her mother's boyfriend being treated like a toddler. Patricia had barely finished talking when Nicky asked about the next steps and whether there was anything she could do right away.

"Whoa, slow down. I'm afraid you'll have to wait until tomorrow." Patricia watched as her daughter's face fell, but then saw her eyes light up as they discussed their plans for the next morning. Funny, Patricia thought, how they were bonding over something as absurd as turning her boyfriend into a virtual infant.

Patricia varied little from her routine in Robert's hypnotic session that night, only reinforcing the concept that a wet bed brought on an affectionate response, and trying to implant the idea that this was a logical way to repair their relationship. It took every effort she had not to push on into new ground, but she knew he wasn't ready for that yet.

The next morning was almost déjà vu, as she woke Robert from his slumber in sodden sheets. This time, though, she made sure she left the door open wide. Just as Robert stood groggily from his bed, his pajamas darkened with his urine, Nicky walked into the room.

"Mom, have you seen my—" she began, stopping in mid-sentence as she froze, staring at the scene before her. "What's going on here, Mom? Did he do what I think he did?" As she started to move closer to the bed, Patricia jumped in, ever the protective girlfriend.

"Nicky, you need to go back downstairs now. Robert and I need a little private time. We'll come down in a few minutes and have a talk."

Nicky nodded, her mouth still agape, as she backed out the door. Patricia began to worry if she could ever trust that Nicky was telling her the truth about anything after that performance.

Patricia turned her attention back to Robert, who hadn't moved. Moisture had formed at the corner of his eyes as he stood stunned that he had been caught in his shame. Patricia took advantage of the moment, speaking to him in the most maternal tone she had used yet.

"Robert, I'm afraid our little secret isn't so secret anymore. We are going to have to go downstairs and have a discussion with Nicky about your problem. Don't worry, I will do the talking, but you do have to be with me. First, though, we need to clean you up. Come along, baby, let me give you a bath."

Robert still hadn't said a word and followed Patricia into the bathroom without complaint, where they repeated the routine of the previous day. Patricia hummed happily as she bathed him, whispered encouraging words into his ear, and touched him lovingly. At one point their eyes met, and Patricia took Robert's head between her hands and gave him a gentle kiss on the forehead. He sighed in response. One thing she did scale back on was her sexual touching. She had an idea that would be taking that aspect of her plan in a different direction.

This time, she led the silent man back out of the bathroom by the hand, pulling his underwear out of the drawer and kneeling down before him.

"Step in," she commanded softly. "That's a good boy, now the other foot."

Patricia pulled his underpants up to his waist, running her fingers along the inside of the waistband as if to measure the fit. She had him sit on the dry corner of his bed as she put on his socks, then handed him his pants to wear while she found a shirt. Once he was dressed, she brushed his hair back with her hands, pretended to help tuck in his shirt, then led him down to the kitchen to the waiting inquest.

Nicky was waiting for them, her face etched in concern and curiosity. Patricia led Robert to his customary chair, gently pushed him into it, then sat down herself. She took his hand in hers as she faced her daughter.

"Nicole, I'm sorry you had to stumble into that this morning. We're always open about what goes on in this family and should have spoken to you about Robert's problem before you discovered it on your own. As you can see, Robert has been wetting the bed at night. It's obviously very embarrassing for him, so I hope you forgive us for not telling you before now."

Patricia tensed slightly before Nicky replied, hoping her daughter remembered how to react. She shouldn't have worried, as Nicky spoke as if she had been up practicing all night.

"That's okay, I understand. If I were peeing myself, I wouldn't want anyone else to know either. Do you know what's causing it?"

"No, not yet. We're hoping it's a phase that he'll grow out of. But until he does, he'll need you to understand that he can't help it and promise that you won't tease him about it."

"Of course, Mom! I wouldn't be that mean!" As she spoke, Nicky circled the table and put her arms around Robert's shoulders in an awkward hug. "Don't worry about it, Robert. I'm sure you will stay dry really soon."

Nicky returned to her seat, then addressed her mother as if Robert weren't capable of participating in this discussion between

43

adults. "But Mom, there is one problem. That's my old bedroom, and my old bed, and sometimes when I have friends over, we sleep in that room because the bed has a trundle. If Robert's been wetting it every night, the mattress must stink pretty bad. It's probably ruined, and we need to replace it. But if we do, how can we make sure he doesn't wet that one too?"

True to their plans, Nicky managed to make her argument sound like she was not blaming Robert for anything, but that she had to raise a problem that needed to be addressed. Still, to any stranger listening in, it would sound like Robert was a mere child. The fact that he hadn't added to the conversation only added to that effect.

"You know, that's a good point, Nicky," her mother replied, as she squeezed Robert's hand and looked him lovingly in the eyes. "I have to be at work in a few minutes and have a busy day ahead. Nicky, why don't you work on finding a solution today and we can discuss what you've found when I get home tonight."

Nicky nodded, adding "That sounds good." She looked at Robert, whose expression reminded her of a puppy that had just piddled on the carpet. "Don't worry, Robbie, I'll figure something out."

With that, she left the table, and practically flew to her room, her part of the mini-drama done for now.

Patricia herself gave a few words of encouragement to her befuddled boyfriend, then quickly grabbed her briefcase, and left, unable to stop smiling broadly all the way to the office. Everything had gone just perfectly. Now the next step, a crucial one, was in the hands of her daughter.

Nicky Joins the Plot

It took all of her self-control to keep within the speed limit on the way home that evening. She really was busy that day. She had told Robert the truth and didn't have time to call Nicky to see how she had done. As she pulled into the garage behind her home, she saw that an old and obviously stained mattress had been dragged out to the alley. Patricia practically ran into the house.

Nicole met her at the door. "It's been perfect. I think he's been too embarrassed to see me today, so he's hardly come out of his office at all. I have everything ready. But..." Nicky cut her mom off just as she opened her mouth to speak, "You'll have to wait until after dinner. You're not supposed to know my solution, so there should at least be a little bit of a surprise."

At that moment, Patricia could have strangled her daughter, especially seeing the mischievous twinkle in her eye, but she knew she was right. Wherever Nicky got her acting ability, it didn't come from her. As painful as it would be, she would have to wait. What she could do, though, was make sure that they ate earlier than usual that night. She rushed upstairs to change her clothes, then began preparing the food.

Dinner was quiet, an awkward silence replacing any conversation. Robert pushed the food around on his plate, barely eating, mistaking the mood as a continuation of the women's hostile attitude to him. Or maybe he was worried that any effort to speak would quickly turn the conversation to his recent troubles keeping the bed dry. He was right to be concerned.

Nicky finished eating first, but rather than bolt from the table or get up to start clearing the dishes, she remained seated, waiting for Patricia to finish. It didn't take long for Patricia to push her chair back and stand up, taking her plate to the sink. Robert seemed to sense an opportunity to bolt back to his study but was stopped short as soon as he made his move.

"Robert, please sit back down," Patricia said sternly, leaving no room for her cowed boyfriend to object. Robert obeyed, avoiding eye contact as he resumed his place. "We need to finish the conversation we began this morning. Nicole, did you devise a solution?"

Nicole's eyes lit up; it was finally her time to take center stage. Patricia only hoped that she wouldn't go all diva on her and overplay her role in this delicate stage of the production.

"Yes, Mom, I did. The first thing I had to do was get rid of my old mattress. I tried to wash out the stain and the smell, but it was no use, it had to go. I hope you don't mind, but I used your credit card to buy a new one." Seeing no response from her mother, she continued. "But we can't afford to replace the mattress every time Robert pees it. I couldn't think what to do at first, but I tried to think it through logically.

"I realized that I had used that mattress since before I was potty trained, yet it still stayed fresh and usable. What was different? I wet myself in my sleep like Robert or any other toddler. Then it dawned on me. First, I remember what a big production you made when I started staying dry at night. We even had a little ceremony, and what did we do?"

Nicky looked expectantly at both Patricia and Robert. Patricia remained stoic and silent, although a slight smile of recognition of where this was headed reached the corners of her mouth. Robert continued to avoid eye contact, his head downcast, his face red.

"We played some music and took the rubber sheet off of my bed. So, I reversed the process. Instead of a little girl going from bedwetter to a big girl, we have a grown man regressing to a bedwetting little boy. Just the opposite, you see? So, I went shopping. When I got back, I went to my old room, that same bed, played some music, and put a waterproof sheet over the mattress."

Here she looked at Robert, who reluctantly raised his head to meet her gaze. "I couldn't find a rubber one, but they had so many cute patterns of plastic sheets at *Babies R Us*! Wait until you see it, Robert. It has baby bunnies and kitties."

Patricia couldn't restrain herself from joining the fun any longer. "Good thinking, Nicky! Robert, please thank her. She came up with the solution all by herself!" As she spoke, Patricia put her hand under Robert's chin and raised his head so that he would have to face the two women. He did not look pleased. Before he could speak, Nicky continued.

"Wait, Mom, I'm not done. While I was putting the plastic sheet over the mattress, something else occurred to me. It wouldn't be enough to just save the mattress. Every morning there will be wet and smelly sheets to wash too. Since you go off to work right after Robert gets up, it would fall to the only other adult to wash them. Me. So I bought something else too."

Robert looked puzzled. He just doesn't see it coming, Patricia thought. For somebody so smart, he really was clueless. She turned back to her beaming daughter.

"Diapers. Did you know that they come in sizes big enough to fit Robert? Not at Babies R Us, of course, but other stores have them. So, I bought some. A lot of them, actually. They are a lot cheaper by the case, so I picked up a couple."

Robert's mouth dropped open as he stared at Nicole, disbelief in his eyes. If only I had a pacifier, Patricia thought to herself, giggling internally. Keeping her straight face on the outside, she continued to praise her daughter.

"Why, I never would have thought of that. Good job!" Before Robert could say a word, she jumped forward. "So, it's settled, then. Robert, before you go to bed tonight, and every night until we can be sure that you've overcome your problem, we'll be putting you into a diaper. That starts tonight. It's getting late now, so why don't you go get ready for our nightly session and I'll be up in a bit? We'll wait until we're done for diaper time."

Robert slunk off to the bedroom, his feet dragging as if burdened by heavy weights. As soon as they heard the door close, Patricia and Nicole dissolved into a giggle fit like they had never had before, trying desperately to keep the noise to a minimum so as not to carry it upstairs.

"That was brilliant, Nicky, just brilliant," Patricia said as she wiped tears from her eyes. "He really is easy to manipulate. All the

47

more reason to protect him from the wiles of other women." Patricia winked at her daughter and then sat back in the chair. She would give Robert a little time to get accustomed to the feel of his plasticized mattress before she would make her way to the room. She had no idea how she'd be able to concentrate enough to put him under tonight.

She closed her eyes and breathed slowly.

Robbie is Diapered

She didn't have to worry after all. The emotions of the evening appeared to drain all of the energy out of Robert, and he fell into a deep trance with very little effort on Patricia's part. Once he was under, she couldn't resist, and pulled a corner of the top sheet up. The happy little baby animals that greeted her almost made her lose it, but it was too important to build on what they had going. She needed to maintain control.

After the by-now routine discussion of Robert's wetting and the affectionate response that would follow, which Patricia cut a bit short, she moved in a new direction.

"Robert, you seem troubled. Is something the matter?"

Robert nodded, then proceeded to tell her about the family meeting without any prompting. He was obviously upset by this new development and expressed his dismay.

"Oh, no, Robert, this is a good thing. A very, very good thing. A most positive step. Don't you see that?" Robert frowned but did not reply. "You see, we have been working on getting Patricia to see you in a much more infantile light. We want her to realize that you could not be to blame for anything that happened with Joyce because you are really helpless in so many ways. And who can't be blamed for anything they do, because they don't know any better? Babies, Robert. Little, tiny babies. They can cry and make messes and act badly in public, but no one blames them because they aren't capable of acting any differently. So, if we can get Patricia to see you in the same way she sees little babies, she will stop blaming you for that whole incident. Do you see, Robert? Does that make sense to you?"

For the longest time, Robert didn't move. His eyes were active, and his mouth seemed to be forming words as if he were talking to himself. Finally, as Patricia stared helplessly, he nodded his head. Patricia exhaled, realizing she had been holding her breath. He bought it. It was a bunch of crap, but in his desperate state, he latched on to this theory in an effort to do whatever it took to get back in her good graces. How sweet, she thought. And how fatal.

"Good, Robert. I knew you would figure it out. And what else do babies do, Robert? They wet the bed. Every night, they wet while they sleep and every morning they wake up soaked. So, they are put into diapers by those who love them so that they can pee all night long but be protected. The diapers are a sign of love, Robert. You should be so happy that Patricia is taking this step."

Robert looked a bit confused but was clearly relieved, as if he had solved a puzzle or a burden had been lifted from him. Now that the idea that diapers were a good thing had taken root, Patricia worked with Robert to reinforce the thought, coming at it from different directions but always with the theme that if he wore diapers and continued wetting, Patricia would see him in the same way she viewed innocent infants. When she ran out of ways to approach it, she began to bring Robert out of his trance.

When his eyes opened and he regained some awareness of where he was, Robert looked at Patricia in a new way. She gazed back, exhausted from their session, not moving nor speaking. It was Robert that broke the silence.

"I'm ready," he said softly.

Patricia had a momentary lapse of memory and couldn't figure out what he was ready for. Then it hit her like a sledgehammer. Of course! How could she forget? She stood up, trying to mask her enthusiasm, and looked down at Robert.

"Why don't you undress, then lie back down on the bed while I go get your diaper," she said in the motherliest tone she could master. As she scanned the room looking for the diapers, she saw that Nicky had been very thorough. Baby powder and lotion and a container of wipes on top of his dresser. A large diaper pail in the corner. Patricia wondered if Robert had seen that. The little girl touches back from

Nicky's childhood. All that was missing was his bottle and bars on his bed, she thought. Maybe in time…

But where are those diapers?

She moved to the doorway and called downstairs for Nicky to come up. Immediately, Robert spoke up.

"Not Nicky, Patricia! This isn't something that she should see. This is just between you and me!"

"Nonsense, Robert," she replied calmly and soothingly. "Nicky is a big girl, she's old enough to babysit. She should learn how to properly put a diaper on so that there are no leaks. And there may be times when I have to work late, or I'm out of town, where Nicky will have to be the one to diaper you. There's no shame in it, dear."

Robert didn't look convinced, but he didn't have a choice as at that moment Nicky breezed into the room. She opened a dresser drawer to reveal two neat stacks of disposable diapers. Taking the top one, she handed it to Patricia.

The two women moved like one to the side of the bed, towering over the now totally humiliated man. Patricia couldn't help but notice that in his embarrassment, Robert's penis had shrunk to almost nothing. She wondered if her daughter had noticed, and a quick glance clearly showed the smirk on Nicky's face.

"Now, honey, it's important to get this right, because a diaper doesn't do any good if you put it on improperly and it leaks. First, you need to position it under his bottom. Robbie, lift up for me. That's a good boy. Now, I think powder is better than lotion because it helps draw moisture away from his skin." As she spoke, Patricia shook a generous amount of powder over Robert's crotch and bottom, creating a small pink cloud in the air above. "Besides, it just has that irresistible smell of baby."

Robert seemed to be trying to pretend he was somewhere else and blocked out her infantile references. "Now you rub it in gently." Patricia spent very little time with this step, not wanting to arouse her boyfriend. Fortunately, there was no response. "Then just pull it up, tug down one side so that it's tight, and pull the tape back. Like that."

In seconds, Robert was firmly ensconced in his first diaper as an adult. If only he would suck his thumb, Patricia thought wistfully.

51

"There you go, Robbie, that wasn't so bad, was it," she said kindly, smiling. "Doesn't that feel nice and comfy and safe? And it will be so much better not waking up in a nasty puddle in the morning, won't it? Come now, Nicole, give him a kiss."

Both women kissed Robert on the forehead, Patricia lingering just a bit and brushing his lips with her own as she pulled back. Robert's face flushed. As mother and daughter left the room, turning out the light and pulling the door shut, Robert sighed and closed his eyes. What he didn't realize was that it was only 9:00 at night, the hour when all good babies should be in bed and the adults in the household got time to themselves to discuss grown-up things.

Patricia wasn't sure if she or her daughter were more excited by the events of the evening. They jabbered quietly and enthusiastically for over an hour, working out the next steps in Robert's training. It would be difficult to wait a few days before progressing, but it was necessary to make sure that Robert began to routinely wet his diaper during the night and become accustomed to being put into one at night. Even harder, though, at least for Patricia, would be the fact that so much of the next stage would occur while she was at work, leaving it in the hands of Nicole.

The next few days dragged on, but the good news was that Robert seemed to react positively to the affection both women showered on him while diapering him and when they found his diaper wet in the morning. Each day his diaper was wetter than the day before, which to Patricia was a sign that Robert was subconsciously falling deeper into a dependency on his infantile protection. She decided to plant the thought in his mind that the wetter he was, the more the women would love him. It seemed to work.

They continued to be cold and distant to him during the daytime hours, and when Robert's temper appeared to be on edge more than before Patricia knew it was time to move forward.

That night, after putting Robert into his now-routine trance, she began to deviate from the conversations that they had been having, which focused on the importance of the nighttime wetting. Her first step was to plant an idea in his head and hope that he thought it was his own.

> "Robert, you've been doing so well at wetting yourself every night, and it has been working, hasn't it? Patricia and Nicole have been very, very nice to you when they diaper you and also when they clean you up in the morning. But I am sensing that something still troubles you. Am I right, Robert?"

Robert nodded slightly and began to open his mouth to speak, but Patricia quickly jumped in.

> "It's the rest of the day, isn't it Robert? It's not enough for them to treat you kindly only in the morning and at night. You need things to go back to the way they were. You need Patricia and Nicole to show their love for you around the clock, don't you? Of course, you do. That's a very understandable thing to want, Robert."

A small tear formed at the corner of Robert's eye, a clear indication that this idea was, in fact, on his mind and that Patricia didn't have to suggest it after all. That would make things easier, and Patricia decided to jump ahead.

> "That is easily solved, Robert. Would you like to learn how to have both women shower you with affection both day and night? Would that be something you want, Robert?"

Robert nodded his head enthusiastically.

> "I thought so. This will be very simple, Robert. You are a smart man, and I think you have probably already figured out the solution, haven't you? Of course, you have. Good job, Robert! You know that whenever they see you as a helpless infant, they forget all of your adult transgressions. Every time that you wet the bed, they smile, they hug you and they show how much they love you. All you have to do to get that same love during the day is to behave in the same infantile manner you do at night. All you have to do is wet your pants. That would be so easy to do, wouldn't it, Robert?"

Robert's expression showed that maybe it wasn't quite the solution he had anticipated or desired. As before, Patricia could see his mind racing as he tried to process what he was being asked to do. On the one hand, he was an adult, but whenever he acted as one, he got the cold shoulder. Only when the women saw him as an innocent baby, not accountable for his actions, did he feel any warmth? Wetting his pants didn't mean he wasn't an adult, and it didn't have to be forever. If it meant Patricia, and even Nicole, not being angry with him anymore, what did he have to lose?

At least that's what Patricia hoped was going through his mind. She remained silent, taking the risk that he would come to that conclusion without any further prompting. It may have only been a few minutes, but the time seemed interminable.

Finally, maybe a little reluctantly, he nodded. Patricia was overjoyed but had to keep her voice as neutral as possible.

"Of course, that was so smart of you to think of that, Robert."

She smiled as she saw Robert's face relax, appreciating the credit she was giving to him.

"All you have to do is wet your pants. Soon, everything will be just wonderful, but you don't have to hear that from me, do you, Robert? You figured it out all by yourself just like a big boy."

Patricia spent a few more minutes reinforcing the idea that wetting his pants may change the women's perspective of his culpability but wouldn't mean that he wasn't a man. The session had gone on about as long as she liked to extend it, but she couldn't resist putting one more thought into his head.

"Robert, I think you should start moving forward with your plan tomorrow morning. Make a trial run. If Patricia or Nicole reacts to your wet pants in a loving manner the first time you do it, then do it again in the afternoon. If you get more love, do it again before dinner. Train them to see you as an innocent baby, Robert. Bring out their love that you know is there by wetting your pants over, and over, and over again."

54

It was then that Patricia heard a slight giggle by the bedroom door. At some point, Nicole had opened it up a crack and was listening in. Patricia quietly but frantically signaled her to leave, then turned her attention to Robert. Slowly she brought him back to the world of the living and left the room to deal with her daughter.

Patricia wanted to be stern about Nicky's uninvited eavesdropping, but any anger quickly faded due to the absurdity of it all, and by the time she met Nicky in the kitchen, they both dissolved in uncontrollable giggles.

"You don't really think that will work, do you, Mom?" Nicole asked when she caught her breath. "I mean, think about what you're asking him to do."

"It wasn't my idea, Nicky, he thought of it all by himself," Patricia replied with a wink. "And yes, I think it will work. Any doubts I had about this whole plan went away that first morning he woke up in a wet bed. Now will it happen tomorrow? Who knows? But you had better be prepared just in case. Don't make plans with your friends for the next few days."

Nicky nodded. For this to work, someone had to be home if and when Robert peed himself during the day, and Patricia couldn't afford to reschedule all of her patients waiting for that to happen. Patricia looked at her daughter, jealous of her freedom to stay at home. What she wouldn't give to be present when Robert walked into the room with wet streams of pee running down his jeans. A thought came into her head, which could be the next best thing. She made Nicky promise to discreetly call her and leave the phone on whenever Robert approached her. Patricia could use an earbud to hear the conversation without raising her patients' suspicions.

To compensate for what she may miss that day, as well as to reinforce the connection between urine and affection, Patricia paid special attention to Robert as she took off his wet diaper the next morning, lavishing him with praise and hugging him at every opportunity. She remained careful not to do anything to arouse his sexual interest, though, due to the part of her plan that she had not so far disclosed - even to Nicky. Before she left the bedroom to head off to work, she kissed Robert lightly on the lips and patted his behind.

As she waited for her first patient, Patricia placed her Bluetooth bud in her left ear and put her phone on silent, being careful to cover her ear with her hair and to place the phone where it wouldn't be seen from the couch. As it happened, her first patient was the bed-wetting teen who had inspired this whole crazy idea. Despite herself, she became engrossed in his latest self-flagellation and time passed quickly.

Her next patient was a no-show, which normally would irritate Patricia but on this day, it allowed her to reflect on the course of events over the past few weeks. Long gone were her internal debates on the ethics of what she was doing, which should have bothered her but did not. No sooner did she begin to drift into thought, though, than her earpiece came alive and she heard Nicole's voice.

"Oh, I'm sorry, Robert, but you startled me. What's the matter, why do you look so sad? Is something wro—oh, my. Did you have an accident? I'm sorry, that's a silly question, of course, you did. Don't cry, it's okay... there, there, really, everything will be okay." Here Patricia could hear the scraping of a chair, presumably Nicky standing up to go comfort Robert. She listened impatiently, waiting for someone to say something. Finally, Nicky spoke again.

"It's alright, Robert, I know you didn't mean to do it. Sometimes things happen that we just can't control, don't they?" Patricia smiled as she heard one of the phrases they had rehearsed. "Why don't we go get you cleaned up and back into some nice fresh undies and then I'll get you a glass of juice and you'll feel all better."

Patricia wondered if Nicky was laying it on a bit too thick. She heard footsteps as the pair left the room, then realized that Nicky hadn't taken her phone with her. She wouldn't be able to hear what happened next. She wished that she had instructed Nicky to call her if anything happened. She waited impatiently for the phone to ring, but it never did. Eventually, her next patient arrived, and she put herself back into therapist mode while still waiting to hear from Nicky. She didn't want to call herself because she never called home and didn't want Robert's suspicions aroused. The day dragged on. When her last patient of the day was ten minutes late, Patricia didn't wait around. She tore home.

Patricia tried to compose herself as she entered the house but was careful to appear as normal as possible. She tiptoed past Robert's closed door and headed straight to Nicky's room, knocking lightly and then entering without waiting for an answer.

Nicky was lying back on her bed, listening to her iPod as she typed on the keyboard of her laptop. Not having heard the knock, she was a bit startled to see her mom in the room but quickly broke into a wide grin as she pulled out her earbuds.

"Mom, you won't believe it. He's wet himself twice today. At least twice that I know about. He's been so embarrassed that it's possible he doesn't even come to me for help every time. It worked, Mom, it worked!"

Patricia sat on the bed next to her daughter, sharing the excitement of the moment. "Well, don't just leave me hanging. Tell me everything!"

Nicky crossed her legs underneath her as she turned to face Patricia. "Did you hear when he came to me the first time? Okay, good. I'm sorry I couldn't take my phone with me when I went to clean Robert up, but I thought that would raise his suspicions. He actually let me take him by the hand and lead him to the bathroom, just like a child! He couldn't even look me in the eye. It was a bit weird stripping off his pants and underwear—I mean, he tries to act like my father— but it was easier once I began to think of him as a real toddler. I did just what we had talked about. The whole time I told him how it was just an accident, how I knew he couldn't help it, and that it didn't mean that we didn't love him. I tried to talk in the same tone of voice that mothers use with their little kids. I washed him up, then led him to the bedroom and picked out a clean pair of underwear for him, then held them open while he stepped into them. I pulled them up and slid my fingers around the waistband, then patted him on the bottom. Same thing for a new pair of pants. He even let me button and zip them! I gave him the biggest hug ever and smiled at him and told him that if he had any more accidents, to let me know. I even said that this would be our little secret.

"He didn't move right away but I think he mumbled 'thank you' while I was leaving the room. Then he shut himself up in his office and even skipped lunch. I don't think he wanted to face me. But a couple of hours later, he was back and this time he was really, really soaked. I was even more sympathetic this time, although I might have called him 'baby' instead of 'Robert' once. Again, I stressed that I knew it was an accident and that there were some things that aren't our fault, and that there was no sense blaming him for it. This time, though, I said that maybe it would be a good idea if we talked to you about it when you got home. He didn't say either yes or no to that. I had to clean off his chair—Mom, that was kind of gross. But I smiled the whole time and had him hold my pail and called him my little helper. I'm sorry, but that part of it was so much fun I couldn't help myself. I think I hugged him more than I've done in the last three years. So that's it. I haven't seen him since."

Patricia leaned into her daughter and took her by the hands. "You were just perfect. Remind me never to get on your wrong side again." They both smiled and sat silently for a bit before Patricia stood. "Well, let me go start dinner. I think we'll have to have another family meeting after we eat." Both women broke into broad smiles, anticipating more fun at Robert's expense.

Robbie Learns The New Rules

The kitchen smelled wonderful as the chicken dish Patricia threw together simmered on the stovetop. As she was setting the table, she sensed a presence behind her and turned to see Robert standing in the doorway. She was disappointed when she noticed the absence of pee stains running down his legs, and wondered why he had come to dinner before he was called. She waited in vain for him to say something, so she quickly decided to take the initiative.

"Robert, I'm sorry, I didn't hear you come in. Dinner won't be ready for a few minutes yet, but that will give us a chance to talk for a bit." As she spoke, Patricia moved closer to Robert and put her hand on his arm. "Nicky told me that you've had a bit of a rough day. It's okay, I know it's not your fault. Sometimes acting like a grown-up is too hard. I know that I've been hard on you for the past few weeks, but I'm beginning to see that maybe I was expecting behavior from you that you aren't quite ready for. There's still a little bit of a child in you in some ways, and I think that's part of what I find attractive about you. So, when a mature woman tries to manipulate you..." here the irony of what she was saying made it hard to keep a straight face... "you just weren't able to see what was going on. I can't blame you for your innocence. You just didn't know any better. Now, is it all right if I check your underpants to see if you stayed dry since your last accident?"

By this time, Patricia had her arm wrapped around Robert's shoulder and her breasts were rubbing against his shoulder. Robert hadn't said a word yet, and he stood frozen on the spot. If she hadn't been so close, Patricia might not have seen the subtle nod in response to her question.

Sliding down so that her head was level with Robert's crotch, she unbuckled his jeans, pulled down the zipper, and lowered his pants to his knees. A slight thrill passed through her as she saw that the front of his underpants was damp and yellowed. That would make it so much easier for what was to come.

"Oh, Robert, you're wet. That's okay, I think we caught it before you soaked your pants. We still need to clean you up before dinner, is that okay, sugarplum? Nicky!" she called as she caressed the side of his face with her hand."

In seconds, Nicky was by their side. "Could you please stir the chicken for a few minutes while I take care of Robert? It won't take long."

Nicky's gaze fell on Robert's midsection, resulting in a small smile. A quick glance at her mom reminded her of what she should do. "Robert, did you go pee pee in your panties again? I'm glad you did, really. This way our Mommy will see for herself that you are having trouble staying dry and we can all find an answer to the problem together." Wooden spoon in hand, Nicky took a few steps to Robert's side and gave him a kiss on the cheek. "Now don't dawdle. Dinner is almost ready."

Patricia wanted to be angry with her daughter for pushing way beyond what they had discussed saying, but Robert didn't seem to even notice that he was being talked to as if he were three years old, or if he did, he accepted it. Ten minutes had gone by and he hadn't said a word, and even now was silent as Patricia took him by the hand and led him to the bathroom.

Once there, though, he broke down in sobs. "I'm sorry, Patricia, I don't know what has come over me. I'm so, so sorry... for everything."

At that moment, Patricia knew dinner would be late. It was time for the talk that in some ways would open the door to success in her plan, but one which she had in other ways been dreading. She would have to choose her words carefully. She guided Robert to sit on the toilet and then took a seat herself on the edge of the bathtub, taking his hands in hers and looking him straight in the eye.

"Robert, I know the last few weeks have been difficult for you. They've been hard on me too. I miss how close we were. But what happened between you and Joyce, rightly or wrongly, bothered me immensely. You may not have realized it, but for as long as we've been together, I've been insecure about our relationship. For one thing, you're much younger than I am. I know, only six years, so maybe it's irrational, but in the back of my mind, I've often wondered if you would be happier with someone closer to your own age. Also, men that are so sweet and attentive and, hopefully, devoted are rare. Nothing has come easy to me in my life, Robert, so it has always nagged at me as to why I've been so lucky to find you. I've always been waiting for the other shoe to drop.

"So, for as long as we've been together, I've been worried about losing you to another woman. When you told me about what happened with Joyce, it seemed like my worst nightmares were coming true. And I had to know what was going on in your mind. I still don't have all of the answers, and I want our nightly sessions to go on for a while yet, but I can tell you what I've discovered so far. Don't take this the wrong way, Robert, but in one important way, we are so much more than six years apart. I've heard boys mature more slowly than girls, and I think you are the textbook example. There is so much about life that you address in much the way a child does. No, don't look so upset. I think that's a good thing. It gives you a sort of innocence, a purity of thought, that most adults don't have. When I analyzed our relationship, I concluded that it's a fundamental basis for why I love you. You really aren't equipped to deal with issues that face grown-ups, so how can I blame you if you don't act in an adult manner? It's not your fault if you haven't matured enough yet to know how to put off a sex-starved vixen, now, is it?"

Patricia smiled warmly at Robert. "This will sound strange, but it took your wetting the bed to drive that point home to me. In some ways, I will always see you as an adult and as my equal, but in other ways, you are closer to my child and that's a good thing. I want to take care of you, to watch over you. When I see you in the morning in your wet, droopy diaper, I feel an overwhelming sense of warmth that only reinforces the adult side of my love. I don't ever want you to lose your innocence, Robert. Now of course, that doesn't mean that at some point you won't grow out of your bed wetting or," Patricia paused slightly as she squeezed Robert's crotch, "your pants wetting. But they don't bother me, Robert. In fact, I think it's kind of cute."

Weeks of pent-up emotion seemed to suddenly rise to the surface as Robert's eyes met Patricia's, and he broke down in a gusher of tears and sobbing. Soon, Patricia too was crying and they held each other in a lingering hug until they each began to regain control. After a few more minutes, they stood in unison and Patricia began her motherly task of cleaning up her child. Nicky entered at that same moment to see what was keeping them from dinner, and she pitched in. Soon the trio headed out the door to dinner, hand-in-hand-in-hand.

The Next Step In Robbie's Regression

For the first time in weeks, there was conversation at dinner. Instinctively, Nicky knew to focus on subjects completely apart from wet beds and pants. She related a story about a friend of hers who got set up on a blind date only to find it was her brother, and soon everyone at the table was laughing. Everyone felt good, but the elephant still hadn't left the room.

As the last of the food was consumed and everyone sat back, sated and happy, Patricia knew she had to bring reality back into the fold. "Nicky, would you please put on water for tea? We need to talk about how to address Robert's problem."

At first, Robert's face fell, but Patricia's warm smile and her reaching out to take his hand seemed to give him some comfort. As Nicky poured tea, his face relaxed and Patricia knew that he would have no objection to the solution that had already been decided upon.

Patricia spoke first. "Robert, there's no reason to be embarrassed about what's been going on with you. These things happen, and Nicole and I are here to offer our support and to help in any way necessary. Isn't that right, Nicky?" Nicky nodded as she gave Robert a big smile.

"The only thing that is bothersome is the fact that your accidents, if they continue, will result in a lot of additional laundry and may mean having to keep cleaning up your chair, or our couch, or whatever else you're in when you wet yourself. The very nature of accidents means you can't control when or where they will happen. In fact, it just now occurred to me—what if you wet yourself while we were out to dinner, or shopping? How will we make sure that doesn't happen?"

Everyone knew the solution, but Robert looked so sheepish at that moment that the women knew he wouldn't be the one to propose it. Nicky spoke up.

"Well, we can't control what we can't control. Robert doesn't know when he is going to pee himself, so we can't ask him to hold it until it's more convenient to wet his pants." Patricia almost lost her composure and kicked Nicky under the table. "But what we can control is containing his urine so that it doesn't go everywhere. Diapers work so well for his bed wetting, I think he should try using them during the day as well."

Patricia managed to look as if the idea hadn't occurred to her. "Why, that's an excellent suggestion, Nicky. What do you think, Robert? We could at least give it a try unless you can think of a better solution."

Having planted the idea that she thought Robert's diapers were cute, added to her efforts during the hypnosis sessions, Patricia was sure that Robert would go along. And he did. He even gave his verbal "okay" along with a nod of the head.

Patricia smiled. "Fine, then, that's settled. Nicky, would you please clear the table and do the dishes? I need to go take care of Robert."

Nicky's look of disappointment was tangible, but Patricia knew that if everything worked out, she would get more than enough chances to diaper Robert. Patricia took Robert by the hand, then worked her arm around his waist, pulling their bodies together as they walked to his room. She talked to him softly and with affection as they covered the short distance, telling him how proud she was that he could address his problem so maturely.

Once they were inside the bedroom, Robert reached to unbutton his shirt but Patricia stopped him. "Just relax, Robby," she whispered in his ear, "let Mommy do it."

Slowly, almost seductively, she undid each button, keeping their torsos close. As she slid the shirtsleeves down Robert's arms, she made sure to brush his chest with her own, lingering just long enough. Her goal was to show affection with just a hint of sensuality, without going far enough that he would become aroused.

64

Once the shirt was disposed of, Patricia took off each of his socks and then removed his pants, moving a little more quickly while being careful not to allow it to become sexual. She pushed him gently to a sitting position on the bed, then sat down herself so that their bodies touched. Turning Robert's face to hers with her hand, she kissed him lightly on the lips. The look in his eyes was one of a man that would do anything for this woman who must love him so much.

"Let's get your diaper on, then we'll have our session a little earlier tonight. I think we're almost to the point where we won't need to have them as often. Lately, your behavior has made me think that maybe you really can be trusted, that your behavior with Joyce was just one of those situations you aren't big enough to handle." As she spoke, Patricia made sure she was holding the diaper where it would remain clearly in sight as Robert watched her speak. With luck, her reference to his behavior and wearing diapers would become associated in his subconscious mind.

Patricia hummed randomly as she diapered her boyfriend, frequently smiling and making eye contact. When she was done, she propped a pillow under his head and proceeded to put him into his trance.

When he was ready, Patricia wasted no time.

"Robert, you seem to be in a much better mood tonight. Did something happen?"

Robert did, in fact, seem to be devoid of any of the usual agitation that he showed in these sessions. He briefly, and somewhat incoherently, brought Patricia up to date on what had happened. If Patricia hadn't participated, she might not have made sense of what he was describing. She decided to take the lead.

"That is such good news, Robert! It appears that your idea to wet your pants during the day has done exactly what you had hoped it would! Patricia associates your infantile behavior with innocence and is beginning to trust you. Agreeing to wear daytime diapers was brilliant, Robert. That way she has something physical to remind her of your innocence, even when your pants are dry. I think it would help if you left your pants off at home, don't you? That way

65

every time she looked at you the idea would be reinforced, and her trust would continue to grow."

Patricia hadn't planned on drawing Robert in that direction, the idea just slipped out. She liked it, though. She liked it a lot. She decided to press on, just a bit.

"I'm glad you agree, Robert. Plus, that will make it so much easier for the women to see when you need changing. Because if you want them to really see how childish you are, you shouldn't tell them when you are wet. Mommies and sitters know to check their babies. Babies don't tell them. Nod if you agree, Robert."

Robert hesitated for just a moment but did nod. Patricia took a deep breath, exhaling quietly. She hadn't planned on planting this suggestion tonight, but it seemed a natural place to do so. Worth the risk.

"Then logically, you can see what else you should do, don't you, Robert? Of course, you do, you're only a baby when it comes to toileting, but you're a very intelligent man otherwise. So, I knew you would figure this out. If you want Patricia to continue seeing you as an innocent man-baby, and you know how cute she thinks you are in your diapers, and you're not going to even bother telling her or Nicole when you need to go potty, then you know what that means, don't you, Robert?"

Clearly, he didn't as a puzzled frown crossed his face.

"Of course, Robert. That's it exactly. Babies don't just pee in their diapers, do they? They go poo-poo too. So, if you want Patricia and Nicky to really believe that you can be trusted, that you are as innocent as a child, then you need to do everything in your diapers. They will expect that, Robert. Going number two in your diddies will be the behavior they expect from a baby. They will love you for it."

It took a long time to get Robert to follow that tortured logic and to agree to it, leaving Patricia exhausted. She looked at the door as she began to bring him out of his trance, relieved not to see Nicky there. Patricia hadn't told her that she would be taking things this far, nor why. She smiled. Nicky was going to get a somewhat unpleasant surprise if this suggestion took hold.

Once Robert was awake, Patricia sat next to him on the bed, gazing into his eyes, patting his diaper, and smiling affectionately. They remained like that, every bit a loving couple, for a long time before Patricia kissed Robert on the forehead, turned out the light, and tiptoed out of the room.

Robbie Becomes A Real Baby

Later that evening, while sipping a glass of wine, Patricia began to have second thoughts about keeping Nicky in the dark about the direction she was taking Robert's training. For one thing, it really would be unfair to surprise her with a dirty diaper if Robert took the suggestion from that night's session. More so, though, she would need Nicky to perform what she might consider an inappropriate, or even disgusting, act in order to bring Robert to his final stage. But Patricia had given this a lot of thought, and she wanted... no, needed... Robert's behavior modified, for her own mental health and to strengthen their relationship.

Patricia sighed. This would not be an easy talk. Nicky was aware of the circumstances of her conception, at least. When she turned fifteen, Patricia was sat her down and told her everything. It had been an emotional evening, full of tears and accusations, and finally hugs and a sort of catharsis. They were both glad that the big secret Patricia had carried for so many years had finally been brought out in the open. Still, the topic had never been discussed again since that time.

Patricia stopped by the kitchen on her way to Nicky's room to pour her daughter a Coke. Stalling a bit, she thought to herself. Carrying her own wine and Nicky's drink in her hands, she made her way down the hall.

Nicky didn't seem surprised to see her and curiously asked how their session had gone. Patricia answered vaguely, then sat on the bed next to her daughter.

"Nicky, I know I've been asking a lot of you as an accomplice to this whole weird plan of mine, although I think you've actually enjoyed it." Nicky's broad grin affirmed this assumption. "But what I'm about to ask of you might be going a bit too far. I need you to be honest with me, and if you don't think you can do this I absolutely will understand and won't hold it against you. You'll have to forgive me if I need to talk a bit to lead up to my request."

She had her daughter's rapt attention. Patricia briefly referenced their conversation from a few years earlier, deliberately avoiding going back into detail. She could see Nicky's concern growing and wanted to get to the point. To the fun stuff, at least from her own point of view.

"What I didn't talk to you about before, and what is still hard for me to say, is that the incident leading to my pregnancy has left a few scars. Most notably, and I can't believe I'm telling my own daughter this, is that it is very hard for me to be intimate with a man. For me, sex is something to be tolerated when necessary but will never be enjoyable and if I could avoid it altogether I would. Don't get that look of pity in your eyes, young lady. If that's what I have to trade off to have you in my life, it's worth it."

By this point, both women were close to tears. Time to lighten the mood. "With Robert, it hasn't been that big a deal. In fact, you've seen him during diaper time. It really isn't that big at all." Patricia giggled a bit and, despite her obvious puzzlement over where this was headed and the awkwardness of hearing about this from her own mother, Nicky couldn't help but join her. "Really, I barely feel him inside of me. And just when I'm wondering when he is going to enter, it's over. I don't even have time to dwell on my issues with the sexual act." Both mother and daughter were starting to lose their discomfort, and Nicky obviously enjoyed being brought into her mother's inner, and very adult, circle.

"But Robert's diapering had given me an opportunity that I didn't anticipate when we started down this path. I hope you don't lose respect for me, Nicky, but it opens a door to allow Robert to meet his sexual needs, although maybe not in a way that he would choose while taking penetration out of the picture. It's a way that I can keep him in my life without having to endure the emotional upset of having sex." Patricia stopped to catch her breath, wondering what could be going through her daughter's head right now.

"Okay, that's the background. You've seen how impressionable Robert is, and how open he is to the power of suggestion. How many other men would allow themselves to be talked into pissing

70

themselves? I want to try to take advantage of his vulnerability from another direction, a sort of Pavlovian conditioning. Last night when he was under hypnosis, I suggested that he should do more than just wet his diapers. Yes, Nicole, I want him to start using his diapers for everything."

Nicky must have been aware that her mouth had dropped open, as she self-consciously and quickly shut it. Before she could say a word, Patricia continued. "Yes, that would mean that you would be changing dirty diapers. I understand that it would be an odorous and unpleasant task. I don't look forward to it either. But it would also mean that we have met our goal. Not many women would consider making advances on a man who wears and wets diapers, but there might be a few that would risk it if they were horny enough. But a man who poops himself, whose skin has been encased in stinky diapers for so long that it emits that unmistakable odor even when clean? Who would do that?"

By this point, Nicky was trying unsuccessfully to avoid dissolving into fits of laughter. She was nodding as she rocked back on the bed, obviously enjoying the picture of Robert with a load in his bottom. Patricia smiled, but this still wasn't where she needed to be.

"There's more, Nicky. I want to condition Robert so that the only time he can get hard, the only time that his body is willing to enjoy any sexual satisfaction, is when he is wearing a wet and dirty diaper. There is no woman alive that would be willing to make love under those conditions. Talk about a mood killer. Plus, I think I know women well enough that any sexual feelings they had would quickly morph into a single thought: this poor baby needs a clean diaper. They would stop seeing him as a man and he would forever more be a helpless infant in their minds.

"Maybe you see where this is going. The only way this will have a chance of working is if Robert begins to associate wet and dirty diapers with sexual excitement. We need to make sure that every change of a wet diaper is clinical and maternal. But whenever he has a dirty diaper, he needs to achieve orgasm. What I'm asking you to do when I'm not around, and please tell me if I've lost my mind, is to stroke him through his stinky diaper until he cums. Then just finish the diaper change as if nothing unusual had happened."

71

Patricia stared at the floor, unable to look Nicky in the eyes. As much as she had felt uncomfortable when she had debated bringing Nicky into this, actually verbalizing it felt much worse. She decided to backtrack. Still focused on the floorboards, she added, "Nicky, I'm sorry. It was wrong of me to ask that of you. I needed your help for that to work because he would have to cum at every messy diaper change and I won't always be here. But it was selfish of me, and I hope you forgive me."

Patricia finally got the nerve to look up in Nicky's direction, and she was startled by what met her gaze. Nicky was smiling ear-to-ear, tears from her silent laughter still lingering in the corner of her eyes.

"Mom, I think that is absolutely brilliant. Really, really sick, but brilliant. Don't you know that I love you and that I would do anything to help you out? Well, maybe not anything. But I would love to do this. He's not my real dad, you know. And I've always felt a little guilty about how I came into this world. If I can help save you from your demons, of course, I'll do it.

"But..." and here Nicky moved closer so that their faces were only inches apart... "you owe me. Dirty diapers? Yuk!"

No sooner had Nicole finished speaking than the two women fell into each other's arms in a spontaneous hug. Soon they were happily jabbering about the finer points of bringing on an orgasm through the thick layer of a diaper, including gross ideas about what to use for lubricant if necessary. Patricia was happy to state that Robert was always so quick on the trigger, it probably wouldn't be necessary. By the time she crawled into her bed at a late hour, Patricia fell into the most relaxed sleep she had had in years.

Part of her hoped that Robert would wake up with a bulging bottom so that she could address the first messy accident herself, but he was merely wet, and she disposed of that change with kindness but no overt affection. Of course, Patricia realized that all of the talks she and Nicky had had would be useless unless he actually took to the suggestion she had planted. It would be a lot to expect results this quickly.

As before, Nicky promised to keep her phone ready to speed-dial her mom if the situation warranted. Patricia kept her earpiece in as she listened drowsily to her first two patients of the day. She eventually forgot it was there and was startled when she heard Nicky's voice in her ear. However sleepy she had been earlier, she was alert now.

"Good morning, Robert. Did you want an early lunch? Coming down for a snack? No? Is there something I can help you with? Do you need to go to the bathroom? You have a diaper on, Robbie, I don't mind if you use it. Oh, I see, now I understand. Certainly, let's go to the bathroom and I'll take your diaper off so you can go poo-poo. Come on, take my hand. Is something the matter? Robbie, come on before you—oh dear. Go ahead, baby, you might as well finish now. It's okay, no need for tears. That's what diapers are for. Babies use them for everything, so you don't need to be embarrassed. Come here, let me give you a hug."

Patricia was so engrossed with what she was hearing that she almost forgot that one of her patients was on the couch. Fortunately, Samantha Hawkins repeated the same story in the same way every session, week in and week out. Patricia already knew it by heart.

She could hear Nicky consoling Robert and letting him know that using the diaper for all bodily functions was natural, even expected, and that she and Patricia would have been surprised, even disappointed, if he hadn't. Patricia was glad that they had talked the night before and decided on an approach that would seem both supportive and affectionate, subtly reinforcing the idea that pooping his diaper was the right thing to do.

Patricia realized that Samantha was coming to the point in her narrative where she wrapped things up and fled the office, so her attention turned briefly to her patient. As Samantha closed the door, Patricia focused back on what was happening at home. She heard footsteps, as they were obviously going to Robert's room. Nicky had clearly found a way to bring her phone with her without raising Robert's suspicions.

"Lay down on the changing pad now, Robbie, and let me take care of that nasty diaper. Whew! You are smelly, aren't you? That's okay, it's like baby perfume. I don't mind a bit. Are you wet, too? Let me feel your diaper there." Patricia closed her eyes. Here it was, the moment she had both been hoping for and dreading. She listened intently as she waited for Nicky to continue. What she heard instead was the rustling of plastic. Soon Nicky was humming a little song, occasionally telling Robert what a good boy he was being for laying so still for his diaper change. It wasn't long, perhaps less than a minute, before the sound of plastic being manipulated was punctuated by muffled, male grunting.

Patricia was on edge waiting to hear Nicky's next words, which came almost immediately. "Okay, Robbie, let's open up your Pamper and start getting you all fresh." Patricia couldn't believe it. By dropping the code word "Pamper" into the sentence, Nicky was letting her know that Robert had, in fact, ejaculated. True to their plan, Nicky didn't say a thing that would indicate to Robert that she knew what he had done.

The rest of the diaper change was business as usual, except it took a bit longer and Nicky didn't even try to hold back on the baby talk while she cleaned and re-diapered Robert. As far as Patricia could tell, Robert remained silent, probably worried that Nicky would see the extra discharge in the front of his diaper. Fat chance, she thought, with the little amount he produced.

Finally, she heard Nicky give Robert an exaggerated kiss on the cheek and the sound of one set of footsteps, indicating Nicky was leaving. It was only a moment later that Nicky's voice came back on, louder than before.

"Mom, are you still there? Mom, it was so cool. He actually came to me to ask permission to take his diaper off to use the toilet! Like I'm the adult and he's the child. I thought your suggestion hadn't worked until he squatted right in front of me, made a potty face, and shit himself while I watched! He turned so red! After that, he really did act like a toddler and let me take total control. And you were right. Just a little squeeze here and there and he started bucking right there on the bed. I pretended not to notice. Did you hear? Mom, it couldn't have worked out better."

Patricia sighed in relief as Nicky continued. "But, Mom, it was kind of disgusting. The dirty diaper, I mean. But I guess we'll get used to it. And if I have a baby someday, there's no way it will be as big a mess as Robert, so I'll be prepared."

Patricia laughed and praised Nicky but had to get off the phone as her next patient arrived. The rest of the day crawled, but Patricia used her breaks to clear her next week's schedule. She was going to be home, in person, to make sure that this breakthrough didn't go to waste.

Patricia hadn't been home for five minutes when Robert asked for a talk. He clearly wanted to relate the details of his accident to her before Nicky did. Hesitatingly, he told her what had happened, although the part about Nicky waiting too long to bring him to the bathroom was not in line with what Patricia had overheard on the phone. Rather than challenge him or get angry for his little fib, she let it slide. If he needed an excuse for now, so be it.

"Robert, I don't know why you're upset. Really, I guess I kind of assumed that as long as you're wearing diapers full-time, you wouldn't bother to take them off when you needed to go potty. In fact, I like the idea that you're comfortable enough with them that you don't mind using them for everything. And sweetie, it gives me a chance to spend some extra time with you when I change you. Some special time." Patricia put her hand on Robert's thigh as she completed her sentence, and looked at him with what she hoped were her sexy eyes. She had never been good at flirting.

Robert appeared to consider what she was saying and nodded slowly but not convincingly. Once again, Patricia decided she needed to take the initiative. "Robert, I know the last few weeks have been difficult for both of us and while I'm delighted that we are starting to resolve our issue, I think we could spend a little more time together. I've arranged to take next week off so that we can push through any remaining issues, and I can be here to help you when you need me. Since tomorrow is Saturday, that gives us the next nine days. Would you like that?"

Robert's eyes lit up and he threw himself into Patricia's arms in a giant hug. As they embraced, Patricia couldn't help pulling the waistband of his diaper back and sniffing the air. Nothing.

"I'm glad you are looking forward to it as much as I am, Robbie. I'll tell you what. For now, since you've had a bit of a rough day, why don't we do our session early, right now? You know how much they relax you, and it will be a good start to the weekend."

Patricia didn't expect any opposition and got none. Robert had been able to drop into a deep trance quickly now, and that left more time for the suggestion part. Patricia used it all to reinforce the thought that diapers should be used for everything and to remind Robert that the more infantile he acted, the more innocent he would appear. As she started to bring him out of his trance, Patricia was sure that she had gotten through to him. If there was any doubt a few seconds later, as she awoke him, it vanished in the odor of a newly-soiled diaper.

Both Patricia and Robert were momentarily stunned and neither moved nor spoke. Patricia broke the stalemate by sniffing the air before moving to Robert's side, pulling him to a stand, and then cupping his rear end. Triumphant inside, she stayed calm on the outside.

"It looks like my baby needs his diaper changed. Don't worry, baby, Mommy will take care of everything."

Patricia spread the changing pad down on the bed, then lowered Robert to a prone position on top of it. She smiled at him as she stripped his socks off, and almost as an afterthought took his shirt off as well. Sitting beside him, she gently rubbed his chest, tweaking his nipples, and kissed him on the stomach. Their eyes met, and there was no doubt that Robert was enjoying the attention.

Patricia kept it up for a little longer, noting at some point that Robert had closed his eyes and was concentrating on her touch. She took that as a sign to move down his body, and soon she was playing with his penis through the front of his diaper. With her other hand, she moved the mess sitting against his rear around, trying to strengthen the link between what sat there and what she was doing on the front side.

It wasn't long before Robert began to pant, biting his lip in the sign Patricia recognized as the last step before orgasm. Sure enough, two seconds later his hips rose into the air, and he made a guttural noise. Patricia continued rubbing both front and back until he appeared to have finished. She slid closer to his head, planting a wet and passionate kiss directly on his lips. Robert sighed happily.

The first part of her job complete, Patricia turned her attention to finishing the diaper change. Despite having changed her daughter thousands of times, she wasn't prepared for the mess an adult could make. Resisting the urge to gag, she smiled at Robert as she used wipe after wipe to clean his bottom, with more than a little more time devoted to his penis. After what seemed like an eternity, she placed the tightly wrapped diaper into his pail and quickly spread a fresh diaper underneath him. Traversing the room to the dresser, Patricia grabbed the bottle of sweet-smelling baby lotion and squirted a generous portion into her hands. Beginning with his now-flaccid member and moving to his rear, she massaged the lotion into his skin. For a minute, she thought he might cum a second time. Pulling the sides of the diaper up quickly, she taped him in and again leaned down to kiss him.

"I need to get dinner started. It's late. I'll call you when it's ready."

Patricia didn't look back at her boyfriend as she left the room, but she had never been more confident in an assumption. In the last ninety minutes, he had crossed the line. He was her baby now, and he would be in diapers for as long as she decided to keep him in them. Which in her mind, might be forever.

Patricia spent the next week reinforcing all of the suggestions that she had placed into Robert's subconscious. At the same time, she began to allow their relationship to return to normal, leaving behind the cold persona she had affected whenever Robert's pants were dry. It didn't seem to matter as far as the use of his diapers. In fact, she became convinced that he wasn't even aware anymore when he was urinating. At the very least, a wet diaper didn't seem to be cause for alarm. Robert never asked for a change anymore. He allowed the women in his life to check him and never protested if they put a finger inside the front of his diaper or pulled the back out to smell him.

It was Nicky who noticed the other important development. While Patricia made it her own job to handle every dirty diaper change, as she was able to make them a little sexier than her daughter, about a week into her time off Robert managed to soil himself while she was at the grocery store. Nicky noticed the telltale odor from the other side of the house and chose wisely not to wait for her mother to get home to change the baby. When she took Robert's hand to lead him to the bed for a change, she couldn't help but notice the bulge in the front of his diaper. The very act of pooping himself gave him an erection. The imprinting was a success.

To test how successful, later that night Patricia put on her sexiest nightie and snuggled up close to Robert, whispering naughty thoughts into his ear. As far as she could tell, there was no reaction from his groin. A couple of days later, while they were out to eat, a baby at the next table filled the room with the fragrance of her soiled diaper. Thinking it might be Robert, Patricia surreptitiously began to put her hand down Robert's diaper under the table. He wasn't messy, but he was hard. Even the smell of another infant's dirty diaper caused a sexual reaction. Nothing else, not even a nude and willing woman, would.

Given his lack of interest in sex and the fact that Robert was now functionally incontinent, Patricia chose to keep Robert in Nicky's old bedroom. The infantile odors of powder, oil and, of course, the diaper pail, permeated the room and Patricia had no desire to bring that into her own domain. Robert didn't seem to mind. Over time, Patricia added a changing table to the room and filled the shelves with his diapering supplies. She hoped one day to add crib rails to the side of his bed but didn't want to push too fast.

Robert continued to function for the most part as an adult while in public and with respect to his job but seemed to embrace the life of a toddler at all other times. He seldom wore anything to cover his diaper at home, even when Nicky had friends over, and didn't seem to consider that wearing and using a diaper at his age was anything unusual.

He was happy to have Patricia or Nicky make decisions for him. He remained affectionate and caring in his relationship with Patricia, and she found that she was happier than before to have this combination of man and baby. She no longer had to worry about sexual activity, except for the occasional hand job during a dirty diaper change, although even then Robert frequently seemed to have already ejaculated by the time she changed him. Apparently, he would now cum while in the act of shitting himself.

All was well and in fact, better than ever. Even the relationship between Robert and Nicky had improved immensely, now that Nicky was the one in charge. Only one task remained, a test of sorts. This was so wrong, Patricia thought to herself. But she knew she needed to go through with it.

Patricia let Robert know that she and Nicky were leaving to go shopping for the day, but by arrangement, Nicky stayed behind and hid. As soon as she drove out of sight of the house, Patricia called Joyce.

"Joyce, this is Patricia from down the block. Would you do me a favor? Robert's phone doesn't seem to be on and Nicky is here with me so I can't call her to get him a message. It's important. Would you mind very much walking down to our house and letting Robert know that we got delayed and won't be back home until tonight? You will? Oh, thanks so much."

As Nicky reported to her that evening, Joyce pounced on the opportunity. She must have left her home immediately after hanging up. Not expecting company, Robert answered the door without thinking that he wasn't wearing anything over his diaper. And Patricia had made sure that she "forgot" to change him before she left. Joyce was greeted by a man standing in a drooping, soaked diaper.

Robert realized what was happening when Joyce stared dumbfounded at his crotch. Still, he was unfazed. He invited her in, and she was too shocked to refuse. Nicky said that Robert asked if she would like some coffee but by that time Joyce had recovered and started mumbling an excuse about having to get back, forgetting even to pass on Patricia's message. As she turned to go, however, Robert asked her a favor. Patricia had left without changing him, would Joyce mind? His diaper was getting cold and uncomfortable.

Nicky almost blew her cover as she snorted while trying not to laugh. Incredibly, Joyce consented to change him, probably to see if this was for real. She left soon after, and it was clear that any fire she held for Robert had been extinguished. More importantly, Robert himself had shown that he was willing to let other women care for him, which opened up the possibility of using babysitters. Just in case.

Even better, he apparently now saw all women as caregivers rather than sexual beings.

Patricia returned soon after, giving Robert a big hug. She insisted that the family go out for a celebratory dinner. Robert's inquiry about what they were celebrating was met only with a fit of giggles from the two women, so he let it slide. As the trio left the house, Robert in the lead, Patricia and Nicky gave each other a high-five.

Mission accomplished.

Promises, Promises

Submitted by Jane Doe – published by BBW 1999

Edited by Terry Masters

Summary:

A married man, Dave, is drawn further into the life of a cuckolded and humiliated baby girl, as his wife keeps true to all of her promises.

He'd always been submissive, but his wife turned him into a sissy submissive, then decided he'd be her sissy baby and finally a sissy baby cuckold.

And So It Begins

It was a cold, gray, February Sunday afternoon. Lesley, my wife, pulled slowly into the car park and stopped the car a short walk from the ice cream kiosk. The ice cream kiosk was always open on Sundays. No matter what the weather or the time of year, it would be in this seafront car park, available for ice creams, ice lollies, and other confectionery. Inside, I could see the ice cream vendor, a young female of around 21 years of age. She was probably a student at the local college earning extra money to supplement her grant. She was reading a book to occupy her time, as there would be few customers for her to serve on days like these.

There were just three other cars in the large car park. The cars were empty. Their occupants were probably taking a very brisk walk along the cold, windy seafront.

"Well, what are you waiting for?" Lesley said. My heart was thumping, and my mouth was dry. "Please Lesley, don't make me go for an ice cream," I begged. Lesley looked at me through the driver's mirror. I was sitting in the rear seat. "Button up your coat and get going," she ordered.

I fastened the soft pink buttons of the very childish styled coat that I was wearing. It was pale pink, made from brushed cotton, smocked, and quite short. The kind of coat a six-year-old little girl would love to wear on a Sunday outing with her mother. As I nervously fastened my childish coat, I could see my bare, hairless legs, my frilly anklet socks, and my childish pink patent Mary Jane shoes.

The pale mauve party frock with the masses of white petticoating that I was wearing did not want to be hidden away under the pretty pink coat. Try as I might, I could not hide the fact that I was wearing a little girl's dress. I looked once more at Lesley's grinning face in the mirror. She turned it slightly so that I could see just how ridiculous I looked.

My hair was done in a typical little girl style parted down the center with two wide mauve ribbon bows holding it in bunches. My face was a picture of abject misery because I knew Lesley would not relent in sending me out for an icecream.

"Please Lesley, don't make me go," I begged one more time, hoping for a reprieve.

"If you do not get out of the car this very instant, I promise you, you will be turning up for work tomorrow in that pretty outfit," she stated flatly. I shivered in fear. I knew that whenever Lesley made a promise, she never went back on her word.

"Have you got your money?" she asked, readjusting the rearview mirror so that I could see her smiling face. I opened my hand to reveal the money in my sweating palm, forty-five new pence, all in one pence pieces. "Now go and get your ice cream like a good little girl," she sneered.

The cold winter breeze rushed into the car as I opened my door. The wind blew up my skirts, chilling my privates which were encased in a very frilly pair of flimsy little girl-style drawers. "Close the door" Lesley snapped.

Having gingerly stepped out of the car, I pushed the door shut. Lesley operated the central locking which locked the car with an ominous thud. I was trapped outside. The winter cold enveloped me, and a shiver ran through my body, although I could still feel my face burning with embarrassment.

I walked slowly towards the big white van. The wind blew open my coat, exposing my pretty dress and masses of petticoats which were so short that I had to hold my dress down to prevent my frilly drawers from being exposed.

The ice cream girl was still reading her book as I approached. She looked up as she heard my shoes on the concrete car park surface. Lesley had fitted them with metal taps so I could easily be heard as I walked. I thought her eyes were going to pop out of her head as she stared at me in shock, then amusement.

I stood at the van window, forced to look up to her like a small child because the kiosk floor was higher than the ground I was standing on. She slid open the window, grinning now and shaking her head in disbelief.

"Yes?" she asked, bursting into laughter. I could hardly speak.

"Could I have an ice cream please?" I croaked.

"Any special flavor?" she managed to say in her fit of laughter. I shook my head. "Large or small?" she giggled.

"Small please," I almost whispered, my humiliation robbing me of the ability to talk.

She could hardly get the ice cream onto the cone because she was shaking so much with laughter. She handed down the cornet. I really did feel like a small child reaching up to take the cornet from an adult. I placed the money on the counter, the pennies noisily hitting the hard surface.

"Have you raided your piggy bank?" She burst into hysterics again. I felt my face blush even redder. I waited, shivering with humiliation, as she counted the money into her till. "It's all there," she laughed, still shaking her head. I turned quickly to get back to the car as soon as I could but stopped in horror.

The car had gone.

Panic surged through me as I scoured the car park for Lesley. Except for the three empty cars that were here when we arrived, the car park was empty. I felt tears well up in my eyes. Lesley had left me. I turned around, my hands to my mouth in fear. I had dropped my ice cream. My skirts were blowing up in the wind. My dress, petticoats, and my very frilly little girl drawers were now totally exposed to the ice cream girl.

"What's the matter?" she asked in concern, seeing the look on my face.

"She's gone," I cried, "My wife. She's left me!"

I must have looked like a frightened little girl, standing before her in a pretty frock, wailing about being left alone. A warm sensation enveloped my groin. I shivered as the cold wind found the urine running down my legs while I stood there and wet my knickers. A large pool was soon around my buckled shoes. The girl could clearly see it develop from her position looking down at me.

"You've wet yourself!" she burst out laughing again, pointing to the pool that was forming around my pink Mary Jane shoes.

I burst into tears, real tears of humiliation, shame, and fear. The girl threw her head back and laughed at me as I stood there crying like a child, looking for the world like an upset little girl in ribbons and frillies, surrounded by a puddle because I had just wet myself.

"You'll just have to walk all the way home in your pretty clothes," she laughed, "Unless you want me to ring the lost children's center." She held up her mobile phone. I shook my shamed head, feeling my ribbons brush my face, then turned and walked off.

"Do you want another ice cream, little girl?" she shouted after me as I walked from the car park. I ignored her.

It was five miles to our house from here. I walked as fast as I could. Luckily, the streets were deserted on cold Sunday afternoons like this. A few cars passed and honked their horns, but I just looked straight ahead and ignored their cat calls of "Fairy", "Sissy Boy" and "Pansy."

I felt even colder now that my legs, socks, and frilly drawers were soaking wet. My short frock offered no protection against the biting wind as it blew under my skirts and around my wet privates. No matter how much I tried, I could not stop the wind from billowing out my petticoats, lifting them high in the air. If I held my dress down at the sides, my skirts blew up at the front and back. The opposite happened if I held them there. Oh, how I hated wearing little girl dresses with their short skirts and masses of petticoats.

It was almost dark as I stood at the house door, ringing the bell. Lesley allowed me in, a triumphant grin on her face. Later, after I had prepared and served the evening meal, still in my humiliating clothes, I was told to get upstairs.

"You have been a very naughty little girl," she stated, following me into the bedroom carrying a hard-backed hairbrush, "Dropping your ice cream on the floor after saving up all those pennies."

"I'm very sorry Lesley," I apologized like a penitent child, already nearly crying because I knew what the hairbrush was for.

She motioned me to remove my knickers and lay across her lap. She was now sitting on a chair.

WHACK, WHACK, WHACK, WHACK, WHACK, WHACK, WHACK, WHACK.

She laid into my bare bottom. It didn't take much to make me cry these days and soon the room was full of the sounds of the brush landing on my bare bottom and me crying. Eventually, she pushed me to the floor, where I lay on my back a blubbering wreck.

"Because you have been such a naughty little girl, I have decided to punish you further. For wetting yourself like a baby," she sneered, "I'm going to put you into a baby's diaper."

She took a large white toweling diaper, pink-headed diaper pins, and plastic-lined frilly rhumba pants from the chest of drawers and knelt down beside me. I was still sobbing deeply as she pinned the diaper together around my loins, drawing the frilly baby pants up my legs and settling them over the diaper.

"There, baby is all pinned up in his diaper," she mocked, "And baby can wear his diapers all week." She laughed at the look on my face. "Yes, even at work tomorrow."

"But how will I be able to get my trousers on?" I sobbed. The diapers she had used were extra large, extra thick terry toweling, and very bulky. She shrugged her shoulders.

"That is not my problem," she laughed. "All I know is the diapers and the frillies stay on. If your stupid pants don't fit, you'll go to work with your shirt tucked in your baby knickers," she paused for effect, "And that is a promise!"

I burst into further tears. Those hated words, "I promise!" condemned me to a very humiliating day at work.

She produced a big pink pacifier and pushed it in my mouth, "It's your own fault for wetting yourself," she sneered, "Now get up and let me get you ready for bed."

My party frock, petticoats, socks, and shoes were removed. A very frilly short babydoll nightie and pink booties were put in their place. "As you are now dressed like a baby in your diaper and pretty baby clothes, I might as well treat you like one," she announced. "Crawl through to the spare bedroom. I have a surprise for my little baby girl."

Baby Davey's Nursery

She laughed at my frilly diapered behind bulging from underneath my nightie as I crawled. The spare bedroom had been redecorated. She had turned it into a pastel pink nursery. Dominating the center of the room stood a large pink wooden barred crib.

"You will not be sleeping in my bed anymore," she stated, "Babies sleep in cribs, so you will be put to bed in your crib every night from now on."

"Not every night, surely!" I protested.

"Every night," she laughed, "and that is a promise." She lowered the crib side.

"And as babies go to bed very early, you will be put in your crib at five-thirty every night from now on," she said, motioning me to get into the baby bed.

"But Lesley. What about my squash league?" I whined pathetically as I climbed into the crib.

"Babies do not play squash," she scoffed.

"But Lesley... no... I..." I began to protest again, but she cut my complaints off.

"Do you want me to ring Bill up and tell him the reason that you cannot play squash anymore?" she asked, "Should I tell him you will be safely tucked in your crib all dressed up in baby clothes and pinned into a diaper?"

I shook my head. Bill was the captain of the squash club. "One more complaint from you and I will be straight on the phone," she said, starting to pull the blankets over me.

"Lesley please... no... I have to..." I started to say and immediately regretted opening my mouth.

"Well!!!" she snapped exasperated.

She left the covers, pulled up the side of the crib, then stormed out of the room. I felt completely helpless, surrounded by pink bars wondering what my wife was going to do now. She returned to the bedroom holding her mobile telephone.

"Please, Lesley!" I cried in horror, "I'm sorry! I will not complain again!"

"Too late," she said, pushing the buttons on the keypad. I could hear the ringing tone as Lesley held the phone to her ear.

Please Bill be out, I prayed to myself.

The ringing tone stopped and a male voice answered the call. It was Bill. "Hello Bill, this is Lesley. Yes, David's wife," Lesley spoke into the mouthpiece, walking over to the crib and leaning against the bars.

"I'm afraid David will not be able to come to play squash anymore."

I heard Bill ask, "Why? Is he all right?" He was concerned that I was ill or injured.

"No, Bill, he is not injured or ill. You see Bill, the reason David will not be playing squash anymore is because he will be sound asleep in his crib." She looked down at me. I heard Bill repeat her words incredulously. "That's right Bill, a baby's crib. And just like the baby he is, he will also be wearing a diaper," she told him.

I heard Bill laugh. "You're joking," he said.

"No, Bill. I am not joking. David is in his crib as we speak. He is wearing a diaper, a very frilly pair of baby pants, and a baby's nightie. I am looking at him now. He does look sweet," she laughed. "Yes Bill, you can speak to him. He is crying at the minute. I have had to give him a very severe spanking, so you'll have to excuse his sobbing."

Grinning she handed me the phone.

"Bill, it's me, Dave" I croaked.

"Dave, what is Lesley talking about, is she going mad?" he asked.

"No Bill, she isn't going mad. I'm sorry, but I will not be playing squash anymore." I was sobbing as I spoke.

"What's going on, Dave? You sound like you're crying. Lesley said something about giving you a spanking and you being in a baby's crib and wearing a diaper. Tell me it isn't true, Dave," he said. I could not answer him and burst into tears again.

"It is true, isn't it?" he guffawed, "You're in a crib and you're wearing a diaper and crying like a great big baby." I couldn't talk anymore. Lesley took the phone from my trembling hand and waited for Bill to stop laughing.

"Yes Bill, he is a great big wimp," she laughed along with him.

"What you need is a real man," I heard Bill say.

"Perhaps you could show me what a real man is like," she said suggestively. "Just give me half a chance. The pleasure will be all mine," he responded.

"And mine too, I hope," she giggled like a schoolgirl.

"How about dinner tomorrow night?" suggested Lesley, "I could put something very sexy on, cook us both a meal, open a few bottles of David's best wine, then you could show me just what a real man can do," she said huskily.

Bill was a well-known womanizer. He kept all the guys at the squash club entertained with stories of his conquests, relating in graphic detail how he laid each particular female. I knew Bill only needed the slightest opening and he would be into her panties, and Lesley was making it all too easy for him.

"I'd love to come, but what about Dave?" he asked. Lesley looked down at me and sneered. "Don't worry about him, Bill. He'll be tucked up in his crib by five-thirty, safe and sound in his diapers and baby clothes."

Bill laughed "Can I see him? I can't wait to tell the rest of the guys."

"Of course, you can," she giggled, "I'll put him in a pretty baby dress too if you like."

"Promise?" Bill asked.

"Oh, I promise," she replied, looking directly into my eyes, and another gush of tears ran down my cheeks.

"I can't wait. I will see you tomorrow night then. What time?"

Bill's voice was full of enthusiasm. "Around seven will be fine," Lesley said. "Seven it is then. And Lesley, don't forget to wear something really sexy," he said.

"I won't. It's a long time since I had a real man in this house," she giggled. "Goodbye, Bill. See you tomorrow. Say goodbye to Uncle Bill, baby."

She held the telephone to my mouth. "Bye Bill," I whimpered.

"I'll see you tomorrow in your pretty dress," he guffawed. Lesley switched the mobile phone off.

"You are going to have to learn that when I promise that I am going to do something, I mean it," she stated, showing no sign of sympathy for me as I lay there sniveling in my crib. She lowered the crib side, took a handkerchief, and allowed me to blow my runny nose.

She pulled up the duvet and pushed a big rag doll under the covers next to me. "Now you go bye-bye," she cooed in mock tones as if speaking to a real baby. She pushed the large pacifier back into my quivering lips.

"I want you to consider how much being a naughty little girl has cost you today, David," she said pulling up the crib side and clicking it into place.

"You ARE going to work tomorrow wearing a diaper and frilly baby pants. If your trousers don't fit, you'll go to work with nothing to cover them and everyone will see that you are wearing diapers. In the evening, one of your best friends will be coming round here. He will definitely see you in your crib wearing diapers and a very pretty baby frock," she smiled, "And if everything you've told me about him is true, I'll probably end up in bed with him," she paused.

"Just think David, Bill will be screwing me rotten in the room next door while you're in here, in a crib, wearing a pretty frilly baby dress, a diaper, and sucking a pacifier." She threw her head back as she laughed loudly. "And," she said, once she recovered, "Because you dropped your ice cream today, just as soon as you've saved enough pennies, you will be going back for another one." She made a quick calculation in her head. "That should be in the middle of summer," she giggled, "So you will not have your coat on to hide your pretty dress, and there should be lots of people about to see you. And that is a promise, baby," she laughed.

Her laughing voice faded down the stairs as she left me in darkness in the nursery.

I cried myself to sleep contemplating an extremely humiliating twenty-four hours. I could see Bill in my mind, telling all my friends about me, and I tried to imagine his reaction when he saw me in the crib tomorrow night. Paroxysms of shame coursed through my body. I just hugged my dolly, sucked furtively on my pacifier for comfort, and fell into a very troubled sleep.

Sissy Baby Davy is Exposed

February mornings are dark, and because there was no clock in the nursery, I had no idea of the time. I had had a very restless night's sleep. Strange dreams of people laughing at me and little babies crawling around with my head on their tiny shoulders had caused me to wake several times. Each time I turned, I could feel the hard wooden bars of the crib reminding me that I was sleeping in an infant's bed.

I was wide awake now, and absolutely bursting to go to the toilet. I was unsure of what was expected of me. Should I get up and prepare breakfast as normal, or should I wait in the crib for Lesley to get me out like a child?

My sides ached, and I needed to pee so badly. I decided to get up and make Lesley a really nice breakfast. I really needed to get into her good books. I had just knelt up in the crib, feeling for the catches that held the crib side up, when the door swung open and Lesley turned on the light. I blinked as the bright light hurt my eyes. Lesley was already dressed.

"Diddums babykins have a lovely sweepy time then?" she cooed in syrupy tones. I nodded sullenly. She lowered the crib side. "Bweakfast time precious," she giggled.

"Lesley, I need to use the bathroom," I said, crawling onto the floor. She ignored me.

"Is Babykins going to be a good little baby girl for mommy today," she said sternly. I nodded. I did not want to incur her wrath so early in the morning. "Baby, crawl downstairs for his breakfast then," she snapped.

Reluctantly, I made my way downstairs, finding it a little frightening to take the stairs in this infantile way. She ushered me into the kitchen and watched my face as I spotted the large pink highchair that she had put in the center of the room.

"Up you get, baby," she laughed, patting my frilly padded bottom. "Lesley, where on earth did you get this?" I gasped, climbing into the wooden seat as she held the plastic tray out of the way. "Bernard made it for me," she told me, lowering the tray down and fixing it in place in front of me.

Bernard was the local handyman. He did jobs for all the neighbors, such as decorating, gardening, or fixing things.

"Didn't he ask what it was for?" I asked incredulously. Bernard was a good worker, but he was a "busybody." He knew everyone's business and made sure he related his gossip to anyone that would listen.

"Yes, of course," she giggled, "I told him it was for you." I groaned in despair.

"Put your feet in here," she ordered. There was a piece of wood just above my ankles. It had two semi-circles cut into it where Lesley positioned my legs. Another piece of wood, exactly the same, was hinged onto the first at one end. Lesley brought the two pieces together. Like a set of old-fashioned stocks, they trapped my legs in place.

Lesley slipped a small padlock through a hasp that had been screwed into the edge of the ankle stocks and clicked it shut. She smiled that evil smile when she had me just where she wanted me. I shuddered in fear.

"Put your arm down here," she giggled, pointing to a steel handcuff that was fixed to the side and open, ready to accept my wrist. The steel was cold as she pushed it into place around my arm. Another handcuff at the other side rendered me completely helpless.

"There, now. Babykins is all ready for his brekky," she laughed.

"Lesley, please, I really need to go to the bathroom," I whined, completely trapped in the highchair.

"What are you wearing on your bottom, David?" she asked.

"A diaper," I admitted blushing.

"Tell me, David, why do babies wear diapers?" she spoke with the tone of a schoolteacher talking to an errant child.

"Because they cannot control their bladders," I said weakly. "But I can," I added quickly.

94

"You cannot. You wet your pretty knickers yesterday," she scoffed. "But... I..." I started to say.

"But nothing," she snapped, "Babies wear diapers so they don't get their pretty clothes wet when they do their wee wees. You will use your diaper just like a little baby. And it will stay on until I decide to change it. Your pretty plastic baby pants will make sure it doesn't leak onto your clothes."

I could hold myself no longer. As she prepared a large bowl of rusks in milk, I relieved myself into the diaper. Lesley laughed at my blushing face. She knew I had wet myself.

"Has babykins done his wee wee then?" she mocked. I nodded dumbly.

Lesley tied a big bib around my neck, then while talking to me all the time like a baby, spoon-fed me a bowl of sweet, mushy baby food. A large baby's bottle full of sickly-sweet baby milk followed.

I retched at the taste as I sucked on the latex teat of the bottle, but Lesley made sure I drank the whole bottle. She wiped my face clean with the bib, admonishing me for being a messy baby, and then released me from the highchair.

"Time to get ready for work, David," she announced, ushering me back upstairs.

She informed me that when I was in diapers I could only crawl about the house. I would be allowed to walk only when I had my proper clothes on, or my little girl outfit. She also informed me that she did not intend to change me until I came home from work. She said that she wanted me to get used to the feeling of wearing a wet diaper, telling me that she wanted me to develop a really nice diaper rash.

"I wonder what the young girls will say when I take you to the chemists to get some diaper rash cream, David," she sniggered, "They are bound to ask how bad your diaper rash is. I will just have to pull back your frilly baby pants and diaper to show them."

My normal clothes were given to me on a hanger, and she left me to get dressed, telling me to fold my baby nightie up like a good little girl. I put on my white shirt and tie, gray socks, and then attempted to get my trousers on. It was impossible. The pants would not fasten together due to the bulk of the diaper. I even broke the zipper trying desperately to hide my diapered condition. I was close to tears when she walked in.

"They won't fit," I said, almost in a whisper. "Take them off!" she ordered, "Now get your shoes on." I was still sniveling as she handed me my briefcase. "You cannot go out like that, David. You look ridiculous," she said shaking her head.

"Oh, thank you, Lesley," I gasped with relief, thinking that she had relented on her intention to send me to work looking like this. "Your shirt needs tucking into your knickers," she laughed, "There. That is better."

I almost fainted with shame as she led me to a mirror once she had adjusted my shirt. I looked absolutely ridiculous in my shirt, tie, socks, heavy shoes, and my frilly diapered behind.

"Off you go, David, and have a good day at the office," she laughed, marching me to the front door.

"Please, Lesley," I bawled, tears streaming down my face, "Don't make me go like this." The front door was open now and I felt the cold winter wind on my bare legs.

"Bye bye, David," she laughed, shoving me in the back so I was clear of the doorstep. Then the door slammed shut. I heard it being locked behind me. I stood there trembling with fear, rooted to the spot.

Lesley opened the door. "I suppose I could ring work and tell them you're ill," she suggested. I felt elated at her show of kindness. I dropped to my knees. "Thank you, thank you," I sobbed.

"There will be a price to pay though," she sneered, looking down at me sniveling at her feet.

"Anything," I cried, desperate to be allowed back into the house before anyone saw me. "You had better mean that, David. This is the only time I will break my word, and that is a promise," she sneered.

"I do, Lesley. I will do anything you say," I croaked.

Once inside, she took me back to the nursery and stripped me of my office clothes. "You will be off work all week," she told me, "You're due some holidays anyway. During this week you will act exactly like a baby. Do you understand?" I nodded. "You will not utter one single word that I can understand from now on. You are only allowed to say 'goo goo' or 'ga ga' or any other baby sound you can think of, but no words. Now let me hear you try, and remember you are a baby girl."

"Goo goo goo goo ga," I squeaked. She laughed.

"Not bad for a first attempt. It will come much easier by the end of the week. But I warn you, David, if you talk once like an adult while you are in baby clothes, you will be sorry. And that is a promise."

She put my frilly nightie back on me and made me crawl back to the kitchen where I was put back in my highchair. She only locked my feet and my left arm in the restraints. "I want you to suck your thumb, baby," she said, raising my hand and sticking my thumb in my mouth.

"I want that thumb in your mouth all the time. It only comes out at mealtimes," I was informed. "Goo goo goo," I gurgled, the thumb restricting my speech even more.

"By the time I'm finished with you, sucking your thumb will be second nature," she giggled, "I wonder what they'll say at the office when you can't stop sucking your thumb."

Lesley picked up the phone and rang the office. She informed them that I wasn't feeling too well, and they agreed to give me the week off against my holiday entitlement. "Now baby can stay at home all week with her mommy," she said, pinching my cheek.

"Goo ga goo ga goo," I mumbled.

She was full of herself as she tidied the kitchen up and put the breakfast items in the dishwasher. Once the kitchen was to her satisfaction, she made herself a cup of fresh coffee. I had to have another bottle. While she was drinking her coffee, she wrote a list of items she required for the meal with Bill tonight.

"I wonder what a real man would like to eat," she mused, teasing me. "Should I get him a nice steak, or perhaps oysters? Oysters are supposed to turn a real man on, and I want to make sure Bill is really horny tonight," she giggled.

"What do you think, babykins?"

97

"Goo goo goo," I said dribbling onto my bib. "I'll need some tins of baby food for you, babykins. You are not old enough to eat adult food yet, are you?" she asked, wiping my chin.

"Ga ga ga goo," I answered in baby talk.

She stood behind me and ran her hands in my long hair. I had not had my hair cut for six months now. Lesley had trimmed the ends to keep it tidy, and it was more or less in a "page boy" style.

"Wouldn't babykins look sweet if I dyed her hair blonde and permed it into pretty ringlets?" she laughed. I wanted to say "no" but just continued gurgling like a baby.

"I'll call at the hairdressers on the way back from the supermarket," she smiled putting her coat on, "I'll be able to have your hair nice and pretty for when Bill comes tonight."

I felt tears of frustration and humiliation welling up inside me. "Now don't start crying, babykins. Mommy has to go to the shops to get some things. You stay in your highchair like a good little baby. I'll be back soon," she said, picking up her handbag and the car keys.

She pulled the highchair around so I was facing the kitchen window. "Bernard always cuts the grass on a Monday morning. Remember to give him a wave when he comes," she laughed and breezed out of the back door. I was left alone.

The kitchen clock ticked away slowly as I sat in utter boredom in the highchair. Later, the peace was shattered when I heard the sound of a motor mower start up in the front garden. Bernard had arrived and would soon finish the small front lawn. I knew this nosy old man was bound to look through the kitchen window. I desperately tried to get out of the highchair, but it was futile. Bernard had done an excellent construction job.

I heard the back garden gate squeak as Bernard brought his mower through. Sure enough, his grizzled old face appeared at the window, a broad smile on his face. He waved his fingers as if waving at a child and burst into laughter. I sat absolutely helpless, sucking my thumb. He disappeared and his mower burst into life, drowning his coarse laughter. It was twelve-thirty when his mower stopped, and silence reigned once again. This coincided exactly with Lesley's return.

"Good day, ma'am," I heard him say.

"Hello, Bernard. Would you like to come in for a cup of coffee?" Lesley's voice answered. Surely, she couldn't bring him inside the house, I quailed.

"Love one ma'am. It's bitter cold this morning," he replied.

The lock turned in the door and it swung open. Lesley entered first, grinning from ear to ear. Bernard followed, desperate to get a better look at me in the highchair he had constructed.

"Sit down, Bernard," she smiled at my red face.

"Hello, babykins. Did my big baby miss mommy?" she cooed, pinching my cheek. "Goo ga goo goo," I said in a hoarse whisper.

Bernard could not keep his eyes off of me while Lesley poured them both a cup of coffee.

"My husband is being punished for being very naughty, Bernard," Lesley informed him, sitting next to him at the breakfast table.

"Quite right too, I expect," he laughed.

Lesley told him all about my outing to get an ice cream dressed up as a little girl and how I had wet a very expensive pair of knickers. Bernard was rolling with laughter as she related each detail. "So he is now in diapers," she finished.

"Diapers, a grown man in diapers," he howled.

"Yes diapers, come and look," she said, standing up. She raised the plastic tray as far as it would go with my arm trapped in the handcuff. She pulled up the frilly nightie.

"There you are Bernard, a grown man in diapers." She also showed him the diaper was wet.

"I never! A grown man in a wet diaper!" he kept repeating to himself as Lesley showed him to the door. "You'll be the talk of the neighborhood by the end of the day babykins," she laughed, giving me another bottle feed.

My diaper was sopping wet by the time Lesley decided to take it off me. She put me in a heavily scented bath, washed my hair, and scrubbed me clean. She dried me, then led me over to the white basin where the pink/blonde hair dye had been prepared. She put the wet towel over my shoulder, then started applying the hair coloring. Satisfied that she had put enough on, she sat me in a chair and then proceeded to severely pluck my eyebrows.

The dye was eventually washed out and she towel-dried my hair, sniggering at its new color. Back on the chair, I had to sit still while she applied acrid-smelling perm solution to small strands of hair then put it in the tiniest of rollers. It took well over an hour to put them in. A pink hair net followed. Then I was taken into the nursery and put into a clean diaper. Finally, I was put into my crib for an afternoon nap while my hair dried and Lesley got on with her preparations for the evening.

I did not go to sleep, of course. I just laid there, listening to Lesley as she sang happily to herself. Delicious smells permeated upstairs into my room. I was starving hungry. All I had had to eat so far was the rusks in milk at breakfast and three large bottles of baby's milk.

"Is babykins wide awake then?" she gushed as she entered the room. "Mommy has got babies din-dins all ready for her baby girl," she said, letting me out of the crib and following me as I crawled down to the kitchen.

Several pans were boiling away on the cooker. My mouth watered at the smell. I was soon locked into the highchair. As I was about to be fed, she allowed me to stop sucking my thumb which was already quite sore from being in my mouth all day.

"Is my baby very hungwy?" she cooed.

"Ga ga goo goo ga," I squeaked. The microwave oven bell rang, and Lesley took out a huge plastic bowl of brown mush.

"Here is baby's din-dins," she giggled, putting the bowl on the highchair tray.

She shoveled in a huge spoonful. It was foul and only just warm. I tried to spit it out, only for her to scrape it off my chin and bib and shove it back in again.

"This is proper baby food out of a tin. All babies have this for their din-dins," she said, scraping the bowl as the contents finally disappeared.

"You had better get used to its taste babykins. You will be having food like this for all your meals," she grinned, "And that is a promise."

"Lovely chocky pudding next, babykins," she sang. Another large bowl was put on the tray, this time full of dark brown chocolate pudding. It was sickly sweet, and again I tried to reject it to no avail. I was forced to eat it all.

"All gone, babykins. Who's a clever baby girly then?" she laughed. "Ga ga ga ga goo," I gurgled, glad that the ordeal was over.

Lesley opened a bottle of red wine and poured a large glass. "Does baby want a drinky?" she sang, holding up the glass.

"Goo goo goo goo ga," I gurgled enthusiastically. She took a large gulp of the wine.

"It's a good job I made you a big titty bottle of milk then," she laughed as she teased me. She saw the look of disappointment on my face as she brought over the baby's bottle.

"Babies don't drink wine, babykins," she laughed, pushing the teat into my mouth, "Only adults like Mommy and Uncle Bill are allowed to drink wine. Babies must drink milk so they become big and strong."

The milk was sickly sweet and not at all refreshing, but I was forced to drink the lot. When I had finished, she let me out of the highchair, cleaned my face with a scented baby wipe, and led me back to the nursery.

"I'll get baby ready first, then you can sit on the floor and play with your dolly whilst mommy gets all dressed up for Uncle Bill," she said. She went to the tall wardrobe and pulled out a very frilly baby dress. "Look what mommy's got for her little baby girl!" she said.

The dress was white. It had little puff sleeves and a tiny lace collar. The skirt hung from a high waist in typical baby girl fashion. It was very short, much shorter than my party frock, and frilly, lacy petticoats were sewn into the dress to make the skirt stand out. It was soon over my head, my arms in the puff sleeves, and she had buttoned it up at the back.

She held up a pair of ultra frilly baby pants that matched the dress, removed my rhumba pants, and pulled the new ones over my diapered behind. A pair of frilly ankle socks came next and were put on my feet.

"Look what else mommy has got for her lucky little baby," she said proudly holding up a pair of pink baby shoes in my size. "I saw these in a baby shop window," she said, "They were made bigger for a special display. It was these that gave me the idea of making you into a baby. Aren't they sweet?"

"Ga ga ga ga," I gurgled my reply, watching her fasten them on my feet.

"Now let's get babies rollers out of your pretty hair," she announced. The hair net was carefully removed, followed by the curlers. "Oh my goodness!" she gasped as the last roller came out. She took a length of white ribbon and I felt her tie it tightly at the top of my head. "Fantastic!" she said, "Absolutely fantastic! Come and see what a pretty baby you are, babykins."

I crawled to the full-length mirror and gasped at the transformation. I hardly recognized myself as the overgrown baby girl stared back at me. The ribbon bow perched on masses of blonde curls which cascaded around my face. The dress was ultra babyish in design, so short my frilly drawers and diaper were clearly on view. The frilly ankle socks and baby shoes finished the outfit off to perfection. I hung my head in shame.

"You look adorable babykins," she gushed. "Now hold still while I finish you off," she ordered, fetching her make-up bag.

Pale pink eye shadow, black mascara, and bright red lipstick were applied to my face. "You don't seem to need any blusher," she giggled, dropping the lipstick into her bag. I looked like a baby doll.

Time was getting on. I was sat on the floor in her bedroom and given the rag doll to play with while she showered. She came back into the room wearing just a towel, smelling of really sexy perfume. She dropped the towel in front of me, standing above me naked. She had a beautiful figure, and I felt my manhood start to react inside its toweling prison.

"See what you're missing, babykins," she sneered as she caressed her breasts, "Isn't Uncle Bill in for a treat?" She dressed in a black basque and rolled sheer stockings up her legs and attached them to the suspenders.

"These should turn Uncle Bill on, don't you think so babykins?" she giggled.

"Goo goo goo goo," I gurgled, holding the doll to my breasts.

She sat at her vanity table and carefully applied her makeup. She then took the hair dryer and styled her long dark her. She put on an extremely short, black dress that clung to her slim figure. Four-inch black patent high-heeled shoes completed her outfit. She looked stunning.

"Well babykins, do you think mommy looks beautiful?" she said, admiring herself in the mirror.

"Ga ga ga goo goo."

"More to the point, will Uncle Bill think I look beautiful and want to make love to your mommy?"

She laughed at the absurdity of it. There I was, her husband, dressed in a pretty frock, frilly baby knickers, and a diaper. I was playing with a doll, watching her get ready to get laid by one of my best friends. She found it so amusing that her control over me was so great. I knew that Bill would not only screw her but tell every one of my friends about me being dressed as a baby and make me a laughing stock at the squash club.

Nevertheless, I just sat there on the carpet looking up at her in my ridiculous clothes and my Shirley Temple hairstyle, hoping for her mercy. I had absolutely no chance. She wanted Bill to make passionate love to her. But most of all, she wanted Bill to see me as a pathetic baby girl.

"Just look at the time babykins. It's time for your beddy-byes," she announced. "Crawl into your crib. Mommy will be through in a minute." Dejectedly I crawled into the crib.

As I waited for her to come into the nursery, I tried to summon up enough courage to overcome my submissiveness. I decided that as her husband, I was not going to allow her to let Bill into this house. I knew she would be extremely angry, and I would suffer terribly for standing up to her, but I had to do it.

Lesley breezed into the room. I felt sick trying to get the courage to confront her. She pulled the duvet cover from the crib and raised the side. I was just about to speak when she reached over to the other crib side, unfastened a clip, and pulled a barred lid over the top of the crib.

I watched in horror as it fitted the crib exactly. Lesley quickly locked it in place with two large padlocks. I was trapped in baby clothes in the crib. It had only taken a few seconds. Any thoughts I had of rebelling disappeared as I realized the futility of my position.

Lesley squatted down to my level. "Oh dear, David, you are in a jam, aren't you?" she sneered, "Locked in your crib in your pretty baby clothes. Bill will be here soon, and you haven't even got any covers to hide under," she threw her head back and laughed.

She walked out of the room, leaving me alone in my baby cage. I felt like a condemned prisoner in his cell as time went by slowly.

When the doorbell rang, my heart missed a beat. Lesley had left my nursery door open purposely. I heard her high heels walk down the hall and the front door open.

"Bill. How nice to see you. I'm so glad you could make it," Lesley's voice said.

"I wouldn't have missed this for the world," Bill's voice said, "Jesus, but you look stunning, Lesley."

"Why thank you, kind sir," she giggled, "I bet you say that to all your girlfriends."

I listened as Lesley flirted with him in the hall. "Are you wearing stockings?" he asked, "I cannot resist beautiful ladies in stockings."

"Why don't you find out?" she replied huskily.

It went rather quiet for a few minutes and I imagined his hands running up and down her thighs exploring for suspenders.

"Oh Bill!" she moaned. I then heard them kissing each other loudly.

"Lesley, were you joking about Dave being in a baby's crib last night?" I heard him enquire eventually.

"Certainly not," she laughed, "I've got him all ready for you upstairs."

"I've got my camera with me. Can I take some photos to show the lads?" he laughed.

"Be my guest," she giggled, "Come on. I'll show you where he is."

I shut my eyes in shame as I heard them climb the stairs. "There he is," Lesley said, "My pretty baby girl." I opened my eyes to see them both standing in front of the crib, the room echoing with their laughter.

"Smile, Dave!" Bill said, pointing his camera at me and blinding me with the flash.

He took a dozen photos, and satisfied he had taken enough pictures, he put his camera down. Lesley joined him at the crib side and their arms went round each other's waists as they looked down on me.

"Don't you think he makes the prettiest baby girl, Bill?" Lesley giggled.

"I've got to say that dress really suits him," he guffawed, "The ribbon, the ringlets, those frilly socks, and those cute baby shoes are really you, Dave. I don't think I have ever seen you in clothes that suit you so much." I hung my head in shame, trying my hardest not to burst into tears.

"But there is one thing that suits him more than any other," he added.

"What's that Bill?" Lesley asked.

"His diaper!" he burst out laughing. I burst into tears.

He pulled Lesley close to him and they french kissed, his hands all over her. "Oh, Bill! You're such a real man," she moaned. Bill forced her to the floor. He was soon on top of her, pulling at her clothes.

"Oh, Bill, not in front of the baby," she laughed, looking at me crying in the crib. Her dress was off now. "Baby is much too young to know what we are doing, Lesley. Baby will just think we're playing horsey," he laughed, removing his clothes.

I was forced to watch as he kissed her breasts, then between her thighs. She moaned with pleasure. She returned the compliment. She took his rampant manhood in between her lips. Soon they were making love and the room filled with their rhythmic moans until they both climaxed together. They lay there gasping in each other's arms for a while, then they sat up and looked at me. They both burst out laughing.

"That is what real men do, Dave," Bill sneered, "They do not wear dresses and frilly baby pants with wet diapers underneath."

"Baby girls do, though," Lesley joined in, "Come on, Bill. Let's get something to eat and drink."

"Nighty-night, diddums," he mocked.

"Nighty-night, babykins," she laughed. They turned and left in each other's arms, leaving me in the darkness.

I must have cried myself to sleep for I didn't hear Bill leave. It was also quite late in the morning as it was light outside. Lesley still hadn't unlocked the crib lid. My diaper was wet as I had had to relieve myself in the night, and now I was desperate to open my bowels.

For the last couple of hours, I had fought against soiling my diaper, but it was a battle I couldn't win. Suddenly my willpower collapsed, and I felt the mess squeeze into my diaper and between my legs. It was the most degrading act. It confirmed my status as a baby.

Resigned to Being the Sissy Baby Cuckhold

Shortly after, Lesley danced into the room, wearing a flimsy black negligee with nothing underneath. She looked like the cat that had just had the cream.

"Pooh. Has babykins had an accident?" she giggled unlocking the crib.

"Goo goo goo goo ga," I stammered.

I was told to go downstairs and get in my highchair. She followed and locked me securely into it. The kitchen was full of the smells of a cooked breakfast. My mouth watered as she filled two plates with bacon, eggs, sausage, and beans. She put one plate close to the highchair,

"Hungry baby?" she smiled. I nodded.

"Goo goo," I said in my best baby girl voice.

"Well, mommy will get yours after me and Bill have had ours," she laughed. "Bill! It's on the table!" she called up the stairs.

Bill came into the kitchen wearing one of my robes and kissed Lesley full on the lips. "God you are one sexy lady," he said, patting her bare bottom.

"Get your breakfast before it gets cold," she giggled like a schoolgirl.

He sat down and looked at me. "Coochy coochy coo," he laughed and pinched my cheek viciously. They both ate their breakfasts laughing at me in between mouthfuls.

"Baby has pooh-poohed his diaper," Lesley informed him.

He shook his head in disbelief. "Wearing baby clothes is one thing," he sneered, "But actually soiling himself is another. Do you know, I actually think he enjoys being in diapers."

Lesley looked at my beetroot-red, tear-stained face. "I don't think so," she laughed, "But babies have no choice. They wear diapers whether they like it or not."

Lesley finished her breakfast first, poured some coffee, and then filled my large plastic bowl with baby mush. "What is that?" Bill asked, "It looks revolting."

"It is," she laughed, "It's baby's breakfast."

She took a large spoonful and held it to my lips. "Open wide, babykins," she ordered. I shook my head. She just held my nose until I gagged for air and in it went.

Bill howled as I was force-fed. Lesley then gave me my bottle in front of him. Tears were soon flowing again as they both mocked me for being a great big baby in a dirty diaper. Lesley sat on Bill's knee in front of me, and I watched as Bill's hand slipped in between her inner thighs.

"It's a pity he wasn't at the squash club last night," he said, caressing her sex.

"Why?" moaned Lesley. "He would have found out that we are having a fancy-dress night this week," Bill smiled.

"You're kidding!" she screamed. He shook his head.

"For all members and their wives or girlfriends. And fancy dress is compulsory." They both laughed again at my tear-stained face.

"We'll have to go," she said excitedly, getting aroused again by Bill's attention to her sex.

"Promise?" Bill said, kissing her deeply on the lips.

"Promise!" she moaned, and her tongue plunged into his open mouth.

Bill stood up, picking Lesley up physically as he rose. She clung to his neck, still kissing him. "Oh, Bill! You're so strong!" she gasped. "I'm just taking your wife up to her bedroom to make love to her again, Dave," he triumphantly informed me, "You be a good little baby while we are away."

They left me alone in the highchair, the baby food around my mouth drying hard, my soiled diaper reminding me just what a big baby I had become.

Bill stayed all day. I never saw much of either of them. I was put back into my crib with my doll and rattle to play with. The lid was locked back in place, and I was forced to listen to their lovemaking as I played with my toys. The dirty diaper was not changed either and I could feel a severe diaper rash developing as the acids in my eliminations worked against my skin.

It was early evening when Bill had to go. He came into the nursery and scrolled through the photos he had taken the night before. They both laughed as they flicked through the snaps. "Wait until the guys see these tonight," he laughed.

They kissed again, then Lesley showed him to the front door where Bill promised to call round tomorrow after work.

"I'll make sure I'm properly dressed then," Lesley giggled.

"That nightie will do just fine," he replied, and then he was gone.

At last, Lesley turned her attention to me. I was stripped of my dress, socks, and shoes. Then, in the bathroom, she removed my diaper. All the time she spoke to me as if I were just a baby.

I "goo gooed" and "ga ga" my replies. The scented bath water stung my sore bottom as Lesley scrubbed me. A clean diaper was pinned on me as soon as I was dry, followed by my rhumba baby pants and my baby nightie.

I was fed in the highchair, but she allowed me to lie across her lap to give me her bottle. While she did, she told me what a pretty baby I was and that I was going to be her baby forever and ever. Before she put me to bed, she put the pink hair net over my curls.

"I want to make sure your ringlets are still in for when you go back to work," she said.

The next day we seemed to have more visitors than normal. Bernard had obviously been spreading his gossip. Lesley made them most welcome and did not spare me from their curiosity. I was paraded in front of them dressed exactly as I was for Bill's visit. Oh, how they laughed as I crawled at their feet playing with my rattle and sucking my thumb. After their initial shock of seeing a grown man in such pretty clothes and pinned into diapers, their contempt was evident. For one of the so-called "superior" sex to allow himself to be humiliated in such a manner was beyond belief. They all agreed that I deserved all the humiliation I received at their hands. I had given up my rights as a man. I was a disgrace to the male sex. They also agreed to make sure that I would never be able to claim my rightful position among the male sex again by effeminizing me to a great big sissy boy. I was promised that, by the time they had finished with me, I would definitely not be a man. I would be a baby girl.

I was treated like a doll. They tied and re-tied my ribbon in various positions in my ringlets until they found the place they thought suited me most. My frock was fussed over, and my diapered bottom was patted just like a baby girl. They loved having a "man" in this position and took all their frustrations with the male sex out on me.

Lesley told them of her night of passion with Bill. They all agreed that she deserved a "real man" and volunteered to babysit me if ever she wanted to go out. Mrs. Franklin suggested her older daughter, Jennifer, for the job. She was quite capable of taking care of such a big baby.

I was a whimpering wreck when they all left. I stank of sweet perfume, my eyebrows had been dyed the same color as my hair, and my face was made up with eye shadow, mascara, and lipstick. I lost count of the times I had my lipstick repaired whilst I sat on one of the neighbor's knees. The constant sucking of my thumb had smeared the bright red cosmetic all around my mouth.

Bill turned up later. Lesley had changed into her sexy negligee, ready for his visit. They greeted like lovers, embracing and kissing each other whilst I played at their feet with my doll. Bill told her of his night at the squash club.

"I couldn't get away," he said, "Everyone wanted to see the pictures of him in his baby dress, and I just had to tell them that I made love to his beautiful wife." Lesley kissed him passionately on the lips, her tongue invading his open mouth.

"They have all bought tickets for the fancy dress on Friday. I told them we would be taking him in his diapers and baby clothes."

110

They both looked down at me, laughing at the tears that were running down my cheeks. They talked about me as if I wasn't there, as adults do with babies in the room. Lesley dragged Bill onto the sofa and they cavorted sexually in front of me. I was extremely jealous but felt so impotent in the baby clothes. I just played with my doll.

Over the next three days, I was kept to a strict nursery routine and was supervised by Lesley and the neighbors. Indignity after indignity was heaped upon me. I was introduced to Jennifer, my new babysitter, and two of her friends who found my situation hilarious.

It was totally embarrassing to be sat on a twenty-one-year-old girl's knee, being bottle fed, while Lesley told them all of the baby things that I did - including how I pooed in my diaper. They were given a couple of photos to show all of their other friends.

I also had to suffer the ultimate humiliation of having my diaper changed by Mrs. Franklin. She led me away, with Lesley's permission, to the nursery. I whimpered all the way to the nursery, knowing that this woman I hardly knew was going to deal with my most private of parts. However, I had become so docile that I didn't even think of rebelling and got up onto my changing table like a gentle lamb.

As Lesley had pointed out, babies have no modesty. They are not old enough to get embarrassed when a total stranger changes their diapers.

I felt totally humiliated as Mrs. Franklin lifted my skirts, pulled down my frillies, and removed my wet diaper. She spoke to me throughout the operation, telling me what a dirty baby I was for wetting and pooing my diapers. She spent ages cleaning around my limp privates, amused at the lack of reaction to a female's touch.

"By the time we are finished with you, you will be incapable of having an erection," she sneered, "Your little dickie will never get hard ever again. Its only use will be to wet your diapers."

It was true. The humiliation of wearing diapers and dresses was emasculating me. Even when Lesley attended to me and fondled my private regions, there was not the slightest sexual reaction. She found it so amusing that after only this short time I was incapable of getting hard. What would I be like in a year's time, she had laughed.

Mrs. Franklin pinned me into a fresh diaper, imprisoning the only thing that identified me with the male sex now that I was in such pretty clothes, and covering the diaper with the frilly knickers. "There, now no one can tell that you're anything but a pretty little baby girl," she laughed.

Lesley rang Bernard. She asked him how he was getting along with his latest project. She told him that she required it for Friday if that was possible. Bernard had promised he would do his best.

Friday saw my face made up to perfection. My white ribbon was tied prettily in my ringlets and I was dressed in my baby finery. I wore two thick diapers to emphasize my baby state and a pair of white silk mittens that Jennifer had bought for me. They were tied on my wrists with delicate white baby ribbons. I also had a set of pink baby reins buckled onto my chest. One of the neighbors had found them in their loft. They were of the old-fashioned style with little bells on the front that rang every time I moved. I had to crawl around the house with Lesley holding the leading rein. I was an adult baby puppet on her string.

I was sitting in my highchair when Bernard came. Mrs. Franklin was feeding me a bottle of baby's milk which had a strong laxative powder mixed in. "This will ensure baby poos his diaper in front of everyone at the squash club," she laughed, making sure I drank the very last drop.

Bernard took them outside to view his handiwork. I knew by the cheer that I wouldn't enjoy whatever he'd made. Mrs. Franklin entered the house grinning from ear to ear. A huge black pram followed, pushed by Lesley. I watched in horror as Bernard demonstrated his alterations to the baby carriage.

He unlocked a panel at the handle end of the pram and slid it out. The panel had two half circles cut into it like the ankle stocks that trapped my legs in the highchair.

"His legs fit in this black shopping bag, ma'am, so no one can see them," he said. The large black shopping bag was attached to the body of the pram. "The panel slides back in place above his knees. These padlocks ensure that he can't get out," he beamed with pride at his efforts. "Let's try it out then!" Lesley couldn't wait to see me in it.

Mrs. Franklin released me from the highchair. Bernard held the pram steady, and I treated them to a display of my heavily diapered, very frilly behind as I clambered into the pram. Lesley guided my feet into the bag and made sure my legs were positioned properly in the half-circle pram stocks. She slid the panel into position and padlocked it into place. Bernard was correct. I was trapped. They laughed at my crest-fallen face as I gurgled baby noises.

Mrs. Franklin attached my reins to the body of the pram. "So baby doesn't fall out," she laughed.

There was absolutely no chance of me escaping from the pram. Lesley could wheel me anywhere she liked and, just like a baby, I was helpless to stop her. She confirmed my worst fears.

"I'll take him to mother care tomorrow, and then to the park with all the other babies," she howled.

Mrs. Franklin suggested taking me to school one day to meet Jennifer at home time. Lesley loved the idea. I burst out crying, as I realized that I was now completely at their mercy, and also knew that I would get none. They all laughed at the babified man sitting so sweetly in his pram. Bernard was paid and Lesley asked if it was possible to construct a baby walker for me.

"No problem, ma'am," he said, leaving the laughing females to look after the baby.

As he left, Jennifer walked in. It seemed our house was open to all these days. How she laughed at me in the pram! When her mother told her that she would be wheeling me around to her school on Monday, she jumped up and down with excitement. I was left in the pram for the rest of the day. Lesley had no intentions of changing my diapers before we got to the squash club. She wanted everyone to see that I used my diaper just like a real baby would.

Lesley asked Jennifer to babysit me whilst she got ready for the fancy dress party. She didn't want babykins getting up to mischief, such as trying to escape from his pram. As if I could. Bernard had excelled once again. I was well and truly trapped. The only way to escape from the pram would be to undo the padlocks which were frustratingly out of reach on the kitchen table.

As the time got nearer to going to the squash club, I was having grave misgivings with regard to my situation. How had I allowed myself to be put in this situation? I was sitting in a pram and wearing diapers. I was dressed as a baby girl and even had a ribbon in my ringleted hair.

What little was left of my male pride was fighting back and urging me to rebel. I was a man, not a baby girl for goodness sake. The realization that Lesley was actually going to take me out in the pram dressed as I was and humiliate me in front of all my friends was becoming clearer by the minute.

My male spirit was fighting valiantly against my submissiveness, but it was too late. I was trapped in the pram. There would be no reprieve for me. I was going out in my baby clothes and there was absolutely nothing I could do to stop them.

Lesley breezed into the kitchen. She looked absolutely fabulous and was dressed as a sexy nurse. Her nurse's uniform was so short that her stockings and suspenders were on display.

"What do you think, Jenny?" she twirled to show herself off.

"You look great!" she said, "You'll knock them dead. There isn't a man alive that wouldn't get turned on by you in that outfit." They both looked at me and burst out laughing.

"Well. Maybe one!" They said together.

"Doesn't baby's mommy look super-duper?" Jennifer cooed.

"Ga ga goo goo goo ga," I gurgled.

I nearly died with shame as the young girl raised my skirts and plunged her hand into my diaper and felt my limp penis. She squeezed it, rubbed it, then viciously pinched it with her sharp fingernails.

"No, not even the slightest signs of being turned on," she laughed, "But then again, he is a baby."

Jennifer said goodbye, offering to take me out in the pram tomorrow as school had finished for the week. Lesley confirmed that she could.

"Aunty Jen-Jen will see her big baby tomorrow. Baby go walkies to the park," she cooed.

"Well, David, what a state you are in. All dressed up in your baby clothes, in your pram, ready to go out and meet all your friends who will laugh and laugh at you. You do realize that you will never be able to show your face again to them. They will never think of you as a man ever again. This is the beginning of permanent babyhood for you," she said ominously.

"Bill is moving in with me. He will be the man of the house. You will be our baby girl. I've already written your letter of resignation. I'll take you in your pram on Monday to give it in. I'm sure all the girls at the office will want to see what a pretty baby you make."

I listened in absolute horror.

"Who knows, David? Maybe, one day, Bill and I could get married. Just think, you could be our little baby bridesmaid," she giggled at the thought of it, "And if you're very lucky, we may even adopt you officially."

"But I am your husband," I blurted out.

"Don't be silly," she scoffed, "How many husbands do you know that wear diapers and baby clothes and play with dollies while their wife is making love to another man in front of them?"

She held up the keys to the pram. "I bet you would like these?" she teased. "But we won't be needing these tonight," she laughed, throwing them into a drawer and closing it.

I burst into tears. "It's a good job your make-up is waterproof," she laughed, applying her lipstick, "You seem to be crying all the time these days. But just to make sure that your tears don't ruin your pretty make-up, I am going to make you an appointment to have it tattooed on. Then it will be permanent, and you can cry all you want baby," she sniggered, "And that is a promise."

Lesley took something out of her handbag and approached me ominously. I shivered in fear.

"I thought I told you to talk like a baby when I first put you into your diapers David," she sneered, "It seems that you cannot accept even the simplest of instructions. I never want to hear your male voice ever again. Once I have injected this serum into your throat, David, I never will."

Lesley held up a hypodermic needle full of a clear liquid. "Please don't inject me with that Lesley," I whimpered as she swabbed my neck with a chemical-smelling ball of cotton wool. "I promise I will never talk like an adult in front of you ever again."

"You can't keep your promises David, can you?" she scowled, "But I can, and I promised you that if you spoke like an adult while you were in baby clothes, you would be sorry. As you know David, I always keep my promises. And I promise you now that you will never be able to talk anything other than baby talk ever again."

I squealed in horror as she pushed the sharp thin needle against my throat. "No... No... Please...No... Leslie... goo ga goo-goo ga-ga goo-goo," my words turned to baby gurgles as my throat and voice box froze.

Lesley threw her head back and laughed loudly as I continued to babble like a baby. "It is no use, David. You cannot talk anymore. And guess what?" she howled, "The effect is both permanent and irreversible."

Bill arrived shortly after and nearly had a fit of hysterics when he saw me in the pram and listened to my baby talk. He was dressed as an American Navy pilot, with a white uniform jacket, black trousers, and a white peaked hat. He looked so handsome. He could not keep his hands off Lesley, and they made love there and then against the kitchen door. When they recovered their composure and re-adjusted their clothes, I was given my rattle and my dolly, and a white woolen baby shawl was put over my puff-sleeved shoulders.

"Come on babykins. Let's go and show all your friends just what a big baby you have become," Lesley laughed and pushed the pram forwards. I looked down at myself, my pretty dress, my frilly diapered bottom, sitting in a pram, being taken to be shown off and laughed at by all my friends.

"Lesley, no. Please don't do this!" I wailed. "Goo-goo ga-ga goo-goo-goo gaga," is all that actually spilled from my lips.

"Oh dear, our baby is having a tantrum. I'll have to give her a smacked bottom when we get to the squash club," Bill laughed.

The pram lurched forward. Lesley locked the house door. We were outside. My journey to permanent babyhood had begun. Lesley leaned forward, stuck my pacifier into my mouth, and pushed Jemima into my arms.

"Suck on your pacifier, babykins and hug your dolly. You are going to the squash club to be introduced to all of your friends as our little baby girl," Lesley laughed.

My fate was sealed. There was no use fighting it. I was their big baby girl now and would be for the rest of my life. They could see the resignation in my tear-stained eyes. How they laughed as they pushed me onwards to permanent adult babyhood.

The End

Printed in Great Britain
by Amazon

32993352R00066